DREAMS
—THAT—
NEVER WERE

DREAMS

—— THAT ——

NEVER WERE

GREG MESSEL

Copyright © 2021 by Greg Messel

All rights reserved. No part of this publication may be reproduced, distributed, or transmitted in any form or by any means, including photocopying, recording, or other electronic or mechanical methods, without the prior written permission of the copyright owner and the publisher, except in the case of brief quotations embodied in critical reviews and certain other noncommercial uses permitted by copyright law. For permission requests, write to the publisher, addressed "Attention: Permissions Coordinator," at the address below.

ARPress
45 Dan Road Suite 5
Canton MA 02021

Hotline: 1(800) 220-7660
Fax: 1(855) 752-6001

Ordering Information:
Quantity sales. Special discounts are available on quantity purchases by corporations, associations, and others. For details, contact the publisher at the address above.

Printed in the United States of America.

ISBN-13:   Paperback   979-8-89389-003-7
           eBook   979-8-89389-004-4

Library of Congress Control Number: 2024905773

To friends and school mates who went to Vietnam and never returned... and in honor of those who did come home...

A PERSONAL NOTE

1968 was a pivotal year in my life. I became seriously interested in politics—a passion that still burns in me. The candidacy of Robert F. Kennedy captured my imagination. He seemed to perfectly articulate my feelings about where we should go as a nation. I was enamored by RFK because I believed he would end the war in Vietnam, help the poor, and aid blacks in their struggle for civil rights. I was a senior in high school and living in the San Francisco Bay Area where I had attended several mock political conventions that school year, which fanned the flames of my support for Senator Kennedy.

On the evening of June 4th, 1968, I knew I had to get up early in the morning to take a final exam at Mt. Diablo High School in Concord, California. I should have been studying, but instead I watched every moment of the coverage of the California primary. I kept switching channels between ABC and CBS. My parents and younger brother were all asleep and I was alone huddled near the television watching the returns. Finally the tide turned, and it appeared Bobby Kennedy was going to win this crucial primary. I stayed up past midnight because commentators promised Senator Kennedy would soon come to the ballroom to deliver a victory speech. I looked at the clock. In just seven hours, I had to take my final, but I wanted to see the speech. I was thrilled by his words. Finally, as he concluded by saying "Now it's on to Chicago and let's win there," before flashing the peace sign. I watched Bobby trying to work his way through the crowd to leave the podium. Then I forced myself to shut off the television and go to bed.

In the morning, when I got in my car to go take the test, I heard radio reporters updating Robert Kennedy's condition in the hospital. It was a crushing blow to my innocence and idealism.

— Greg Messel

"Some men see things as they are and say, 'Why?' I dream of things that never were and say, 'Why not?'"

—Robert F. Kennedy

CONTENTS

PART THREE
ARLINGTON

1

CALIFORNIA PRIMARY

Los Angeles - June 4, 1968

On the last day of his conscious life, Robert F. Kennedy felt a profound weariness from the blistering pace of campaigning that he had maintained since March.

In the final days before the California primary, he had whistle-stopped through the San Joaquin Valley; ridden in motorcades, where the massive crowds mobbed him and nearly pulled him out of his car; and faced hostile questioning for hours, both in Watts and Oakland. Some campaign aides had expressed concern in recent days that he appeared to be ill and, at times, couldn't seem to stop shaking.

On June 4th, the day of the California primary, the weather turned gray and gloomy. Kennedy spent the smoggy day relaxing at the Malibu home of family friend and famed filmmaker, John Frankenheimer, who had produced political thrillers like *The Manchurian Candidate* and *Seven Days in May*.

Bobby tried to unwind—swimming, playing in the surf with his children, sitting in the sun, talking to friends, and getting some much-needed sleep. It felt so good to him to escape the frantic campaign that he was considering not going to his own victory party in the Ambassador Hotel downtown. He proposed watching the election results in Malibu.

He was ultimately overruled by his campaign staff, and just before 7 p.m., he arrived at the Ambassador Hotel in Frankenheimer's Rolls Royce. Those in the car that fateful night said Frankenheimer drove "like a bat out of hell" and that most of the conversation in the car was about what would happen after California.

Bobby joined his entourage in the fifth-floor suite to await the results, which had slowly trickled in.

There had never been a year like 1968. America fractured and nearly broke. The Vietnam War continued to deeply divide the nation. More young men were drafted and more died in 1968 than ever before. There were 485,600 American troops in Vietnam as 1968 began. The United States had been involved in Vietnam actively since 1961.

The nation's leaders kept reassuring the American public that the U.S. was winning in Vietnam and there was, at long last, "light at the end of the tunnel." The question, then, that was continually asked by critics became: "How long is the tunnel?"

Meanwhile, the streets of America turned uglier as 1968 progressed. City streets and college campuses were filled with protestors against the war, and black Americans continued their struggle for true freedom.

No one under 21 could vote in America in 1968. Young men, fresh out of high school, were drafted and sent to Vietnam. Many American youth questioned, "Why is it that we're not old enough to vote, but we're old enough to die?"

Senator Robert F. Kennedy, brother of the slain President John F. Kennedy, had calculated he would make a run for the White House in 1972. He initially decided not to run in 1968 against the beleaguered occupant of the White House, President Lyndon B. Johnson. However, with Senator Eugene McCarthy as the "peace" candidate on the Democratic side, Bobby Kennedy changed his mind and announced on March 16th that he would run for president. Then everything changed on March 31, when LBJ went on national television and announced he would not run for another term as president.

Kennedy set a frantic pace to compete in the race and catch up. He was met by wildly enthusiastic crowds everywhere he went. He campaigned in the Kansas primary and won the Indiana primary.

While campaigning in Indiana, on April 4th, Kennedy was informed that Martin Luther King Jr. had been assassinated. Against the advice of his meager security detail and local law enforcement officials, RFK attended a rally in the African-American neighborhood north of Indianapolis. He attempted to console the crowd and urged peace and restraint.

RFK won key primaries in Indiana and Nebraska, but he was upset by McCarthy in Oregon, in a hard-fought battle. The Oregon loss made it imperative that Kennedy win the big prize: California. Polls showed him with a 9-10-point lead over McCarthy, but Kennedy was not leaving anything to chance.

He spent June 3rd, the day before the California primary, in an around-the-clock final push with rallies from San Francisco to San Diego. Polls showed a double win was likely in California as well as South Dakota.

Finally, just before midnight, his victory looked certain. He said to an aide as he left his hotel suite, "How's the food? I have to give a speech. I'll be right back." He took the freight elevator down to the kitchen, walked through the pantry and anteroom, and entered the Embassy Room to wild applause and chants of "We want Bobby! We want Bobby!" About twenty people, including his pregnant wife, Ethel, were on the platform with him.

As Kennedy entered the ballroom, a busboy in the kitchen pantry noticed a small brown-skinned man with bushy hair, looking nervous and anxious, who asked, "Is Mr. Kennedy coming this way?"

The busboy replied that he didn't know.

Sirhan Sirhan crouched by a tray rack near the ice machine and waited.

PART ONE

THE ASSASSINATION

2

THE SHOOTING

Good Samaritan Hospital -
Los Angeles - Wednesday, June 5, 1968

"I think we can end the divisions within the United States… the violence, the disenchantment with our society… We are a great country, an unselfish country, and a compassionate country. I intend to make that my basis for running." Robert F. Kennedy on June 5, 1968

I heard unfamiliar voices talking.

"He's starting to open his eyes," someone said.

"That's a great sign," commented another.

I detected a pain in my side, just below my rib cage. I tried to open my eyes, but they seemed to be glued shut. The voices resumed—talking about me as if I wasn't there. Finally, I blinked my eyes, trying to focus, and soon realized I was in a hospital bed. Standing by me, with concerned looks etched on their faces, was an odd collection of people from my life.

Through my bleary eyes, I saw my ex-wife Brenda; John Greer, my photographer pal from San Francisco; and Darlene Harvey, the reporter from the *Los Angeles Times*, I'd been admiring from afar since I had arrived in Southern California.

Brenda moved forward and tenderly gripped my hand in a way that she had not done for a long time.

"How are you, Alex?" she asked softly.

I gave a weak shake of my head. "What happened?"

"Don't you remember, mate?" John jumped in.

"Remember what?" I mumbled blankly, as my weak voice tailed off into nothing.

"He's still coming out of the drugs. Give him a minute," Brenda pleaded. "They've been keeping him kind of doped up since the surgery. This is the first time I've been able to talk to him."

"Surgery?" I asked.

Brenda shushed me and gently ran her long, slender fingers through my hair. "Take it easy. Don't try to talk right now. Take your time. Then we'll help you understand what happened."

I groggily attempted to get my bearings. "We were at the hotel. Everyone was celebrating Bobby's victory. I was following him out of the ballroom, and there was like a riot. I was suddenly on the floor and couldn't get up. It was strange. All of these people kept stepping on me—on my arms and on my legs."

I glanced at my right hand which was heavily bandaged. "I got knocked down. I'm sorry. Everything is a little hazy. I'm having trouble getting my brain to work."

The three people hovering over me could not have been more different—two beautiful women and John, with his long black hair pulled back in a ponytail and a scruffy beard covering his face. The trio exchanged concerned glances, whispered, and nodded at one another. I started to shift in my bed and was met with a jolts of pain in my side and my leg.

Brenda attempted to lighten the mood. "I was afraid you'd wake up in your hospital bed, see your ex-wife standing over you, and think you'd died and gone to hell."

I gave her a weak smile, while the others chuckled to break the tension.

Brenda was trying to make sure my re-entry was a slow descent, but that strategy was quickly dashed when John started blurting out all the details of the last 14 hours. "Take it easy, Alexander. You've had surgery. You were shot, man. They removed the bullet. The doc says you're going to be fine. Some people from San Francisco are on their way down here, including our boss. Everyone's been worried about you after they saw the news."

"The news? I was shot?"

Brenda glared at John. "Way to go slow, John. Senator Kennedy was shot. You and some other people were also wounded by the assassin."

"No, no, no!" I yelled. "Bobby was shot? No, not this time! This wasn't supposed to happen! Assassin? Is Senator Kennedy going to be all right?"

John moved closer. "Bobby's just down the hall. He's still alive, but he's not doing very well."

"Not doing very well?" I snapped with rapidly accelerating alarm.

John blundered ahead. "This place is like a fortress. It was hard to get in here especially onto this floor. Cops are everywhere."

"Maybe we should go," Darlene said shooting a glance at John. "We'll come back later, Alex. We just had to see you. We were so worried."

"No, no, don't leave right now," I pleaded. I repeated what I had been told to try to take in the enormity of the news. "Senator Kennedy was shot. How could... how did it happen?"

Brenda nodded to John and Darlene. "I'll stay with him. I know you must be very busy."

Darlene leaned over and kissed me on the cheek. She was dabbing tears from her eyes. "It's been a long night. We're all living in a nightmare. I'm so sorry, Alexander. It's good to see you awake."

Darlene grabbed John by the elbow and pushed him towards the door. John flashed a peace sign. "Peace, my brother. I'll see you a little later. Take it easy and get better. I've got to call San Francisco. Everyone's anxious to hear about you."

After they departed, I tried to shift to get a better look at Brenda. She looked great. Her long black hair cascaded onto her shoulders. It was longer than I had ever seen her wear it. She wore a lime green mini dress with white trim and white boots.

"Where am I, and what time is it?" I quizzed Brenda. "Actually… what day is it?"

"It's Wednesday," she checked her wrist watch. "It's about a quarter to two."

"At night? What happened to Tuesday?!"

"You had surgery earlier today, and I just got to town. I came straight to the hospital. I flew down as soon as I heard about the assassination attempt. Your name was on the television as one of those wounded with Bobby. I caught the next plane to LA to see you."

"Uh… wow… that's… I mean, I'm overwhelmed. That's a lot of money. Is that all right with Tom?"

"I was very upset, and Tom immediately offered to fly me down here to see you."

"That's very nice… of you… and your husband."

"Alex, I don't think you've grasped what's going on outside this room. It's a national crisis. I wish you could look out the window at the street below. There are barriers up, and hundreds, if not thousands, of people are lining the street in the front of this hospital. News about the shooting is on TV constantly."

"Where's Senator Kennedy now?" I groggily asked.

"Here. Eric Sevareid and Walter Cronkite have been on CBS saying something has happened to the fabric of our nation. There are signs everywhere that say 'Pray for Bobby.' The raw footage of the shooting has been shown over and over again on NBC. You're right. After the shots were fired, it was like a riot. When I turned on my television, not only did I see Bobby bleeding on the floor in the pantry, but I saw you on the ground with a pool of blood under you. You were wearing a blue blazer, lying on the floor on your side against the wall."

"Is there a television in here?"

"No. I'll talk to the doctor about getting one for you so that you can see the coverage. I know you must be going nuts to be missing such big events. And to answer your question, Tom is fine with me coming down here. I mean, they were talking about you being shot right there on national television. Frank Reynolds on

ABC identified you as a San Francisco newspaperman. I switched channels to CBS, and Walter Cronkite said your name, mentioning you as one of the wounded. The San Francisco television reporters were talking about you giving your bio on KPIX. It scared me. It sounded like you had died."

"Who were the others who were shot? I mean… how many were wounded?" I asked.

Before Brenda could answer, the door burst open, and John and my editor, Phil Cochran, came in, rolling a portable television. Phil ran interference with the nurse, explaining who I was and why I needed to see the television news about RFK. John busied himself plugging it in to the wall and adjusting the rabbit ears so I could see the CBS News coverage and local reporting on KCAL.

"Keep it down," the nurse warned. "We need quiet on this floor. Senator Kennedy and his family are just down the hall. Let's show some respect."

I painfully tried to sit up more erectly so I could see it. We tuned in just in time to see the latest medical update on Bobby Kennedy's condition. As it concluded, I asked John, where Senator Kennedy was shot.

"In that kitchen… ya know…"

"No, no. I mean, physically, where are his wounds?"

John shook his head and looked grim faced. "In the back of his head. I think two shots. Small caliber, but still…"

Everyone seemed to know what that meant, but no one wanted to say.

"But he's still alive?" I asked.

John nodded as he continued to fiddle with the rabbit ears.

Phil had the nurse in the corner talking in muted tones. I heard her say, "Yessir, we can do that."

Phil then rushed to my side. "How are you doing, my friend?"

"I'm hurting. I've apparently only been awake for a short time, and I'm struggling to catch up," I said. "I'm pretty queasy."

"Don't rush it, pal. You've been doing a helluva job. I'm just glad to see you awake and in one piece. Everyone back in our office has

been in a panic about you." Phil turned to Brenda. "Don't worry…
We're going to get you a better situation. We're going to take care
of your guy."

Brenda and I exchanged anxious glances.

"I assume you'll want to stay with Alex tonight. I don't think he
should be alone," Phil said. He kissed Brenda's hand. "Alex Hurley's
a lucky dog."

Brenda blushed slightly and smiled.

"I've got to run," Phil said, pointing to John. "Greer and I have
a lot of work to do. I'm trying to keep the wolves out of your room."

"Wolves?" I asked.

"There are reporters from all over the world trying to get onto
this floor. Everyone wants to get eyewitness accounts of the shooting.
You're a part of history now, Alex. Of course, I want your recollection
of the shooting as an exclusive for the *Associated Press*. Tomorrow
when you feel a little better, let's put it together. We'll copyright it,
and your words and face will be in every newspaper in the world."

I weakly nodded. "Wow."

Phil pushed ahead with his hyper-machine-gun way of
communicating. "One of the people who was wounded was an
ABC News producer. The anchorman, Frank Reynolds, did a live
cut to him. Here's this guy, lying on a gurney, awaiting surgery.
They handed him a mic and said, 'What happened?' That's pretty
hardcore. He's still bleeding, and he's on live television nationwide
trying to report on the shooting."

Phil waved his arm at John, and they headed for the door. "The
nurse said you're doing very well. He just wants to make sure there's
no infection and you're healing properly. Apparently, you also have
some injuries to your leg and hand."

I lifted my heavily bandaged right hand into the air and said
meekly, "I guess so."

Phil continued. "You were trampled by the crowd after the
shooting, right?"

"I dunno. I remember being on the floor, and several people
walked on me like I wasn't there."

John filled in the details. "He had people walking right over the top of him. It was bloody impossible to protect Alex. I couldn't get to him."

"Get some rest, you two," Phil said, as he downshifted from his usual intense persona to his pseudo-sensitive mode. "I'll see you tomorrow."

Both Brenda and I were bewildered by the tornado that was Phil, blowing in and out of my room.

"That's my boss."

"He seems nice," Brenda replied.

"He's all right. He can really turn on the charm."

In his wake, he left a blaring television that had now returned to regular programming after the news bulletin about Bobby. The detective show *The Saint* came on. It showed a man walking down a dark alley, pulling a gun, and shooting it out with some shadowy figures.

"That's the last thing I want to see right now."

Brenda clicked it off. "Would you like to be alone?"

"No, no. Definitely not! Please don't go. Say, Brenda, I'm sorry about all the assumptions Phil just made. You don't have to stay with me. You don't have to be here. I don't know what your plans were…"

"I have a change of clothes in that bag over there. I was anticipating… well… I don't know what I was planning on. The assassination attempt happened after midnight. We went to bed. When we got up to get ready for work, I turned on the TV, and they were talking about Senator Kennedy… and you."

She extended her hands. "This is what I was going to wear to work. Then I just grabbed some stuff, crammed it into my bag, while Tom got me on the next flight to LA, and we were out the door. It was all just an adrenaline rush to extraordinary events. I have no agenda other than to see you. It's not like I was planning to go to Disneyland or anything," she cracked. "Is it all right if I give Tom a quick call on this phone?"

"Of course. Let the wire service pay for it. Thank him for me."

I just closed my eyes and listened to Brenda's part of the conversation.

"Hi, honey…"

"I'm fine, but it's very emotional here. It's so sad. I'm with Alex now in his hospital room."

"Yeah, Good Samaritan. It's the same hospital where they took Senator Kennedy."

"We just heard from a nurse that Bobby is just down the hall. As I walked by the nurses' station, I heard two nurses saying that Jackie Kennedy is here now."

"Yeah… How horrible for her to go through this again."

"Alex is out of surgery. He's awake, and the doctor said he'll make a complete recovery. He's kind of hurting right now and a little groggy."

"Yeah, crazy, huh? Alex was in danger almost constantly in Vietnam and he survived, but now he gets shot in a hotel in LA."

"Alex was shot once. It looks like the bullet missed vital organs, but we haven't talked to the doctor yet."

"We don't know anything about Bobby other than what we can hear on television. This hospital is crazy. There are hundreds of people outside keeping a vigil for Bobby."

"I will. Alex said to thank you for letting me come."

"Yeah, I know. I may sleep on the couch in here just so he won't be alone tonight."

"I will. Me too. I love you so much. Talk to you later." She made a kissing sound before hanging up.

I continued to relax with my eyes closed. My head was clearing, and my memory was beginning to come back. The massive crowds in the ballroom, the stifling heat… All the sounds and the sights of those horrible moments in the kitchen pantry were coming back: the popping balloons… the screaming… the shots… the blood… it was all coming back to me in vivid technicolor.

I opened my eyes when I felt Brenda tenderly rubbing my hair. "Just rest if you need to for a moment. We don't have to talk, or you don't need to entertain me. Do you want to sleep?"

"No. I want to tell you what I saw. It's all coming back to me. Like they say before a color program when the peacock comes on NBC, it's all coming back in living color."

"I'm here for you. It's why I came. I'll stay right here, and whatever you need is what I want to do."

I was quiet for a few moments, and my thoughts turned to Senator Kennedy. "Poor Bobby. It's been one of the best experiences of my life to cover his campaign. It was something real. I watched him tour Watts, Compton, and Oakland just a few days ago. I saw him kneeling down talking to children. I saw him sitting on a curb talking to little black kids about what books they were reading. I saw him embrace a weeping black woman whose son died in Vietnam. I'll never forget some of the things I've seen and heard… and felt." I brushed a tear from my eye. "How could this happen? It wasn't supposed to be this way—not this time."

As I watched her walk across the room, I thought of the words to the song *"The Girl from Ipanema."*

"Tall and tan and young and lovely…"

"We've got all night to talk," Brenda said softly.

"That would be great. I'm still blown away that you're here. I'm so happy to see you. It's been a while."

"You look…I don't know…different. I guess that's what divorce means," Brenda said wistfully. "We're not together anymore."

"Have you had any food?"

"I'm not sure I could eat anything but I should get something on my stomach besides black coffee. The nurse said she could get me a bowl of soup."

The solitude was shattered when the door burst open again, and two hospital orderlies moved towards us. "We've been told to move you to a private room down the hall. Don't move Mr. Hurley, we'll just move your bed. Mrs. Hurley, just grab your personal belongings and follow us."

3

DEATH WATCH

Good Samaritan Hospital - Los Angeles -
Wednesday, June 5, 1968 - 8:30 p.m.

"Senator Kennedy has been shot! Senator Kennedy has been shot; is that possible? Is that possible? It's… is it possible, ladies and gentlemen? It is possible, he has… not only Senator Kennedy, oh my God. Senator Kennedy has been shot, and another man, a Kennedy campaign manager… and possibly shot in the head. Get the gun, Rafer! Get the gun! Get his thumb! Hold him, hold him! We don't want another Oswald!" – On air reporting by Andrew West of KRKD, a Mutual Broadcasting System radio affiliate in Los Angeles

After the swift movement to the private room, Brenda went into the hall and talked to the nurse, while the orderlies made sure I was settled properly into my hospital bed, with IVs, monitors, etc.

When she returned to the room, I apologized again. "Listen, I'm sorry about the Mrs. Hurley business. You've been Mrs. Romano for what… almost two years?"

"Yeah, two years in July."

"Are you still working at Tom's law office?"

She nodded.

"I saw you talking to the nurse. Did you explain our situation to her?"

"No way. Apparently, I get all these privileges because I'm your wife. If I said I was your ex-wife, they might boot me out of here. You know, hospitals. But she told me we can have whatever we want, since my husband was with Senator Kennedy. Your boss assured the hospital they want first rate care for you, and the *Associated Press* will cover it. Pretty nice."

"I've got to take my hat off to Phil, but he probably said all that because he likes the looks of you. He's a notorious skirt chaser. By the way, you *do* look fabulous."

"Thanks. That's very nice of you to say that. I haven't seen you for a while. I've never seen your hair this long. When's the last time you had a haircut?"

I snickered, "I guess I really don't know. Not since I began following Bobby around Oregon and California. Do I look grubby to you, like some long-haired hippie?"

"You mean do you look like your scruffy sidekick? Definitely not. I like your hair longer. I think you look like, uh... Jim Morrison of The Doors. Your light brown hair and blue eyes... I've always thought you looked a little like Jim Morrison anyway, but that's especially true since your hair is longer." She fluffed my hair with her fingers. "It seems like your hair gets kind of curly when it's long. I wish mine did."

"All I need are tight leather pants," I quipped.

Brenda tittered. "You know, I have a ham and cheese sandwich that's supposed to show up soon."

"I hope they bring me one."

"You're out of luck, my friend. You get a bowl of Jell-O and some ice water. Maybe you'll get some chocolate pudding if you're extra good. No solid food for you until maybe tomorrow. Speaking of long-haired hippies, what's the story with your pal, John?"

"First of all, he's a helluva photographer. He'd walk in front of a freight train to get a good picture. It's amazing he's still in one piece. I've seen him in Berkeley, crouching and snapping away, while cops with fixed bayonets and billy clubs charged towards him. He makes a good target when the cops are looking for someone to whack. John *is* a long-haired hippy, but because he's British and talks like the Beatles, he has chicks swarming all over him despite his, to put it politely, his hygiene issues. He didn't spend too many nights alone while we were on the road with Bobby's campaign."

"Ick," Brenda laughed. "He does have a cute accent, like John Lennon."

"See what I mean?"

"I'd better get ready before the food comes." Brenda started to walk away, but suddenly stopped and wheeled around. "Alex! We've got to call your mother and let her know you're okay."

"Would you do that for me? If I call her, it will take forever, and I'm not up to it yet."

Brenda rolled her eyes at me. "You should do it. She's your mother. Besides your mother doesn't like me. And I'm sorry. I said I'd do anything for you, but let me amend that: I absolutely refuse to talk to your father. If I call and your dad answers, I'm hanging up. I don't plan to interact with him for the rest of my life. I especially couldn't take him right now."

"I understand about my dad, but I don't think my mother hates you. Why would you say that?"

"Because when we were divorced she said, 'I never liked you.'"

"Oh."

"Please, Alex. I don't want to talk to her."

"Just tell her I just got out of surgery, that this phone call is costing a fortune, and you can't talk long. Cheap phone bills are a big deal to her. I call her in Walnut Creek, just 20 miles away from my house in San Francisco, and she always concludes our calls by saying, 'Alex, this call must be costing a fortune.'"

Brenda relented and called my mother to let her know I was going to survive. When she hung up the phone I asked, "How did that go?"

"It went."

"I owe you one."

"You owe me a lot more than one, you rat fink," she said with a twinkle in her eye.

"I'm sure she appreciated your call."

"Why do I need a better relationship with my ex-mother-in-law? I get along great with Tom's mother. Why aren't your parents calling to see how you are? Why aren't they standing in this room right now, like I am?"

"All valid questions. I don't know," I said thoughtfully. "But thanks just the same for calling her."

"Your mom asked if they should come down and if you're out of danger."

"What did you say?"

"I said I didn't know if they should come, and all indications are that you will recover."

"Hmmm," I said. "So if I'm going to live, then there's no reason to spend the money, right?"

Brenda shrugged.

"Last year, I was planning to get together with my parents and brother on Christmas day. I was in the East Bay on Christmas Eve working on a story. I dropped by my parents' house to say hello on my way back to the city. Do you know what my mother said?"

"I'm sure I can't imagine."

"She said, 'Since we saw you today, we won't have to go to all the trouble to see you on Christmas Day.'"

"God, I'm so sorry, Alex," Brenda said as she busied herself, putting her small suitcase on the couch where she would make her bed. She looked around for a curtain to pull, but there was none. Lacking a privacy screen, she turned her back to my bed and unzipped her boots so she could pull them off.

My ex-wife has the most beautiful legs I have ever seen on any woman. When she unzipped her mini dress, I was surprised that she wore only small pink panties and no bra. She quickly tied an ugly light blue hospital robe around her. and then took out her hairbrush and began working over her long hair before tying it into a ponytail.

She turned, smiled at me, and extended her arms. "Enjoying the show?"

"Immensely. A bright spot in a thoroughly awful day."

Brenda shook a cigarette out of the pack, grabbed her lighter, and walked towards me. "I'll share if you'd like. I also have a little treat if you need something extra to make it through the night." She took a joint out of the pocket on her robe.

"Are you crazy? When did you start smoking pot?"

"When did I start? Were you under the impression I ever stopped?"

"And when did you stop wearing a bra to the office?"

"When did you become so uptight about everything? I've smoked pot with you, and you've never objected to me not wearing a bra."

"I seem to have enough trouble right now. I don't need to add a felony drug rap to my problems. The whole world is watching this hospital. Cops and G Men are hopping around here like jack rabbits. I don't want to become a historical footnote: the reporter who got busted for smoking weed while Senator Kennedy was… you know…"

"Take it easy. I'll bet the Kennedy campaign staff is tokin' a few joints tonight. This is LA. Do you think you're the only person smokin' grass tonight? I thought you might get a laugh out of it." She sat down gently on the edge of my bed. "Do you remember the last time we were in a nice hotel together?"

"Yeah, you're right. I'm sorry. I'm just kind of unstrung," I said with a smile, trying to regain my composure. Things had been going so well, and the last thing I needed was to start bickering with Brenda.

"I do remember the hotel stay. The only thing different this time is that I have a gunshot wound and you're married to someone else." I inspected the joint. "Is this the kind of grass they smoke at the law firm?"

"Ha, ha. I've learned from the lawyers to never answer a question like that. That's like the question, 'When did you stop beating your wife?'"

I was preparing a retort when the nurse interrupted and entered with the ham and cheese sandwich. Brenda quickly jammed the marijuana into her pocket.

"Where's mine?" I sort of half-joked.

"Maybe tomorrow, Mr. Hurley. The doctor wants to make sure you're healing properly. He'll take a look in the morning," the nurse said wryly. "In the meantime, here's some delicious lime Jell-O and a chocolate pudding. Make sure he doesn't cheat, Mrs. Hurley."

"Yes, ma'am," Brenda joked, and she began wolfing down her sandwich as the nurse departed. "Sorry. I feel kind of guilty."

"Don't."

"Actually, I don't feel guilty. I just said that to be nice."

I began eating the Jell-O with an undersized plastic spoon. "They expect sick people and old people to scrape this stuff out of this tiny cup with this plastic spoon? This could be a game show, like *"Beat the Clock."*

Brenda giggled and continued to chew on her sandwich.

We both were lost in our thoughts while we ate our awful hospital food. I could feel tears welling up in my eyes as I thought about Bobby Kennedy.

"It sounds bad for Bobby, doesn't it?" I asked softly.

Brenda nodded. "Really bad. It was weird watching the news cut away to a press conference right here in this building. You're right. The whole world is watching this place."

"Poor Rosey," I said absent-mindedly.

"Rosey?"

"Roosevelt Grier. You know the 'Fearsome Foursome' of the Los Angeles Rams with Deacon Jones, Merlin Olsen, and Lamar Lundy. They are the best defensive line ever."

"You forget who you're talking to. I don't pay any attention to sports. Remember, that's was one of the things you didn't like about me. Is he a football guy?"

"Yeah, he's a football guy. Well, he's probably six-five and weighs about 290 or 300 pounds, but he's a big teddy bear. When Rosey found out I was from San Francisco, he started teasing me about the 49ers. Anyway, Rosey was one of Bobby's bodyguards. He was fiercely loyal and protective of Ethel. I can't imagine how he feels tonight."

I took a long drink of cold water. "You know, during Senator Kennedy's victory speech…" I had to stop. My emotions overtook me. Finally, I could speak again. "Senator Kennedy joked about

Rosey. He said, 'Rosey promised to take care of anyone who didn't vote for me.' I looked at Rosey when Bobby made that joke, and he was beaming. Everyone was so happy."

Brenda finished her sandwich and chugged the last of her Fresca. "This still seems unreal."

"On Tuesday, it was so exciting. Everyone felt Bobby would win California. Then when he did... I've never felt so much just pure joy in a room or with any group of people. There was spontaneous singing and dancing. Since the vote count was slow, the Kennedy supporters had four hours in that ballroom to build up a good head of steam. When Bobby finally appeared around midnight, the place was in a frenzy."

"The California primary would have changed everything," Brenda commented.

My mind was elsewhere. "It was hot. So damn hot! It felt like I was back in Vietnam. And balloons. I'll never feel the same way about balloons."

"What do you mean?"

"Balloons were all over the ballroom before the shooting. They were in the way... and the pop, pop—the popping was unsettling. Behind the smiles, everyone was afraid—afraid something like this might happen to Bobby..."

Brenda studied my face. "When the shooting started, did you think it was the balloons?"

"Actually no. I grew very sensitive to the sound of gunfire when I was in Vietnam, but when we left the ballroom, I'm not sure I remember hearing the first shot. But still... instead of being festive, the balloons seemed to put everyone on edge. At each campaign stop, it was an unspoken fear; it seemed imminent or fateful. You wondered, is today the day that someone takes a shot at Bobby? I didn't really believe that it was inevitable, but it seems true now. Everyone thought about it when the crazy crowds were so out of control and mobbed Bobby. It wasn't unavoidable; it just happened."

"You know, I read something in the LA paper that disturbed me," Brenda interjected. "A man who was a friend of Bobby's, and

I think a journalist, said when he saw Kennedy lying on the floor, there was kind of a sweet accepting look on his face. It was like, on some level, he knew it would all end this way. I wonder if that's true?"

I nodded in understanding and continued, "A couple of days ago, Bobby was standing on the trunk of a car, driving slowly through a big crowd. The crowd mobbed the car, and they were pulling on him. He had one bodyguard who was an ex-FBI guy, Rosey, and a third bodyguard: the Olympian Rafer Johnson. The three of them had to lock their arms in a human chain, holding onto Bobby so he wouldn't fall, as the crowd pulled on him."

"Wasn't that dangerous?"

"Very. I was talking to Bobby after the motorcade. I noticed his arms and hands were all scratched up and his shirt was ripped in several places. Everyone wanted him to be more careful, but someone in the press corp told me Bobby felt like his brother did. JFK once told Jackie, 'If someone wants to shoot me from a window, nobody can stop it.' Bobby didn't want to be surrounded by security. He wanted to be able to touch people and let them touch him.

"It was made worse after Martin Luther King was murdered in April. It seemed to make the atmosphere became more ominous—more dangerous. We worried about the crowds but James Earl Ray had a hunting rifle and killed Rev. King from a long ways away. It was like Dealy Plaza. The ghost of Dallas hung over us. On the last day, the final day before the primary, we were at a rally in Long Beach, and this guy was heckling Bobby. He kept yelling, 'Who killed your brother?'"

"Oh, no! How did he react?"

"He didn't. RFK kept talking, but it was really bothering all the people in his entourage.

"I remember a motorcade in Chinatown in San Francisco when someone threw a string of firecrackers out into the street as the motorcade passed by. We all gasped. Ethel grabbed her chest in fright. I remember seeing Bobby. He was just a few feet away from me. I saw his face, and I could tell the firecrackers unnerved him."

Brenda clicked off the overhead light. It was a welcome relief to me to just have the indirect lighting in the room. "Do you feel like talking about what you remember? We don't have to…"

"No, I'd like to talk. It might help me remember."

"Would it hurt you if I was beside you in the bed?"

"No. I'd like that very much. Help me get all these tubes out of the way."

Brenda gingerly crawled into bed. "My husband—that's Tom I'm talkin' about—is a patient, understanding man, but he does have his limits. So, mister, don't forget we're not married any longer."

I grabbed my abdomen, trying to re-enforce it, while I laughed. "Ouch… Don't make me laugh. You're totally safe. Between the abdominal surgery and all these tubes…"

"I'd never under estimate you, especially in that department."

I grabbed my stomach again as another laugh shot pain through my lower body. "Stop it. You're killing me."

She propped herself up on her elbow and studied my face, resetting the mood. I got to look into her catlike blue eyes. She rubbed my cheek. "Tell me what happened."

We talked for almost two hours. I told her everything I could remember but also everything I felt. We were both crying as I finished my account. The room was totally silent for several moments as we reclined together in the subdued light. Brenda checked her watch. "Let's turn on the TV and see if anything has happened."

Brenda clicked it on and ABC came up. The "bulletin" screen was on.

"Oh no," I gasped.

Veteran ABC newsman, Frank Reynolds, suddenly appeared and began speaking solemnly, just as Brenda turned up the volume.

Reynolds said, "Robert Kennedy is still unconscious at the Good Samaritan Hospital in Los Angeles. It has been 17 hours since he was shot."

It had been 11 hours since Bobby had surgery to remove the bullets and bone fragments in his head. His condition was described by the hospital as "extremely critical condition." A second bullet was still lodged in Senator Kennedy's neck, but it was said to not pose any immediate danger.

I instinctively looked at my wrist for a watch that wasn't there.

Reynolds was about to continue, when he suddenly stopped talking and grabbed his earpiece. ABC News cut to a podium and makeshift press room somewhere in the hospital.

Kennedy's press aide, a stricken looking Frank Mankiewicz, strode to the podium. I held my breath. *Had Senator Kennedy died?* Mankiewicz looked so sad, and his pallor appeared ashen. In better times, I found him to be a man of great humor. He had always been so nice to me as a greenhorn on the political trail.

Mankiewicz said doctors were alarmed Senator Kennedy had not shown any improvement in the "post-operative" period and that there would be no further medical bulletins until morning.

It was crushing that this could have happened to Bobby, but my heart was also breaking that I wasn't in the press room getting updates from Mankiewicz. That was where I belonged.

Some news stories are important. This was history.

We dozed on and off through a fitful night before we gave into exhaustion. I slept in the hospital bed, and Brenda was under a blanket on the couch. Several times, just as I had finally gone sound asleep, a nurse would come into the room banging things around and adjusting the tubes running into my arm and side.

In the morning, as Brenda staggered to the bathroom, she clicked on the television near my bed. Mankiewicz was at the podium. I held my breath waiting for his first words. He read a statement:

"I have, uh, a short… I have a short announcement to read, which I will read, uh… at this time. Senator Robert Francis Kennedy died at 1:44 AM today, June 6, 1968. With Senator Kennedy, at the time of his death, were his wife Ethel, his sisters Mrs. Stephen Smith, Mrs. Patricia Lawford, his brother-in-law Mr. Stephen Smith, and his sister-in-law Mrs. John F. Kennedy. He was 42 years old. Thank you."

4

WIDOWS ON A PLANE

Good Samaritan Hospital - Los Angeles - Thursday, June 6, 1968

"On this generation of Americans falls the burden of proving to the world that we really mean it when we say all men are created free and are equal before the law. All of us might wish at times that we lived in a more tranquil world, but we don't." – Robert F. Kennedy

Mankiewicz's announcement hit us like a punch in the stomach. Any glimmer of hope we had in our hearts was suddenly snuffed out by the grim reality of the moment that we sensed was coming. While he was still breathing, I hoped, by some miraculous means, Bobby would recover.

"You know, all is lost," I bitterly declared. "All hope is gone. Bobby's the only one who could bring us together. I saw it. I saw it in the faces of the people who rushed towards him. Do you think that's gonna happen with Nixon or Humphrey? We're done for now."

Brenda tried to comfort me with a peck on the cheek. "I know. I know," she said quietly.

Brenda peeked out the door of my room to see what was going on in the hall. I watched her face for a reaction. She hesitated, then whispered, "I'll be right back."

When she returned, I was struck again by how dazzling she looked. She had on a paisley mini dress with swirls of orange, red, and green and her white boots. *How could I have ever let her out of my life?*

When Brenda returned, she was precariously juggling two styrofoam cups of hot coffee and had a wad of newspapers under her arm.

"Coffee and newspapers! That's my girl," I said.

She just smiled as she carefully got the coffee to the table top without spilling a drop.

"What's it like out there?"

She rolled her eyes and shook her head. "It's eerie. All the people we saw yesterday down the hall are gone. It's very quiet—creepy quiet. There's two tough looking guys out there in the hall. I was self-conscious about the clicking sound my boots made as I walked down the hallway. They watched my every move."

With good reason, I thought. I looked down and shook my head. "Too bad those guys weren't in the kitchen when we needed them."

Brenda plopped the Los Angeles daily papers on the bedside table. My elation to dig into the stack of newspapers was short-lived.

Both front pages hit me hard. On the *Daily Mirror* I saw, for the first time, the awful picture of Senator Kennedy lying on the floor in a pool of blood. Someone had their hand behind his head lifting him up slightly. I'll never forget the look on Bobby's face. It was an odd mixture of bewilderment and panic. The banner headline above Bobby's photo was "GOD! NOT AGAIN!"

In a box below the photo was a promo for the *Mirror's* coverage of the shooting. It said, "John Pilger, the *Mirror's* Journalist of the Year, and George Gale, the *Mirror's* columnist, were in the hotel. Pilger's report is on the Back Page. Gale's is on Page 2."

The *Los Angeles Times* was slightly more subdued. There was a banner headline above the masthead that read: "Photos of Kennedy Shooting." The all-caps headline which they often referred to in journalism school as "war declared" headlines, simply screamed "KENNEDY SHOT" above the same photo of RFK on the floor of the kitchen pantry.

The announcement of Bobby's death came too late to make the morning papers.

I flipped through it quickly and saw a couple of bylines by Darlene Harvey. There were more photos. One photograph showed the normally tan and smiling Ethel Kennedy, in a light-colored sleeveless summer dress, now looking grim bending over her wounded husband.

There was a photo showing Rosey Grier wrestling the gun away from a man named Sirhan Sirhan. I didn't see any pictures of me on the floor. There was one of a woman who was apparently hit by a stray bullet from Sirhan Sirhan. She appeared to have a head wound and was being wheeled out of the hotel on a gurney.

I hungrily read the accounts of the shooting, which helped fill in some of the blanks in my recollection.

The photo of Robert Kennedy sprawled on the floor, with a pool of blood under his head, was the saddest thing I've ever seen—yet I couldn't take my eyes off of it. I continued to study the front page, and I saw Brenda watching my face with concern.

You have to be a newspaperman to understand this emotion. Nothing hurts a reporter more than getting scooped. I was on the front line of the campaign with Bobby. As I followed the senator out of the ballroom, I was on my way to file my story, which would include my reaction story about the California primary victory, including an interview I had with Senator Kennedy, as well as his speech in the ballroom. The victory appeared to be his ticket to the convention in Chicago.

The California victory put Kennedy well past peace candidate Eugene McCarthy in the delegate count, 393-258. Vice President Hubert Humphrey had 561 delegates. Kennedy got 2,305,148 in the popular vote in the California primary, but it was still going to be a struggle for him to overtake Humphrey.

Simply put, I wanted to get back into the game. The biggest story of my professional life was developing at breakneck speed, and I was marooned in a hospital bed.

My ravenous consuming of the newspapers was interrupted by the entry of my doctor. He had silver hair and bright blues eyes, and was a tall, commanding presence. After all, this is Los Angeles—he looked like a guy who'd play a doctor on a weekly series on television or a game show host; I couldn't decide which.

"How are we doing?" he asked.

"I've certainly been better," I replied.

"Are you having pain?"

"No… well, I mean, yes… it's just… it's all of this," I said pointing to the newspapers strewn around my bed.

"This is a very, very sad day," the doctor said. "I've never experienced anything like this. Regardless of your political stripe, I think everyone at this hospital feels like there's been a death in the family."

His attention then turned to Brenda sitting in a chair showing plenty of leg in her mini dress which was distracting the doctor. "Who might this be? Your wife or girlfriend?" he asked.

Brenda bailed me out and quickly downshifted the conversation. "Wife. How's he doing doctor?"

"He seems to be doing very well. All of his signs are good. We were lucky. The bullet made a clean entry and a clean exit, just passing through some fatty tissue and missing vital organs. Such a wound can really spill a lot of blood and makes things look worse than they are. That being said, it's never good to lose that much blood. Gunshots are a very tricky business."

"I was back in San Francisco, and when I turned on my television, I saw Alex lying in a pool of blood…" Brenda commented.

"Good God. That must have been horrible for you. I don't need to tell you that a few inches to the right could have yielded a very different result. Gunshots can be like that sometimes. I'm going to get a blood transfusion scheduled for you."

Brenda and I looked at one another and nodded.

The doctor continued. "After Senator Kennedy was shot, Sirhan Sirhan kept firing the gun while it was being wrestled away from him. There were bullets flying everywhere. It was a very dangerous situation in a small confined space. Mr. Hurley and the others who were wounded were fortunate. We have a couple of head wounds, but— I wish we could have..." his voice broke. "...could have done more for Senator Kennedy."

After a moment of silence, I asked, "When can I leave?"

"I'd like to keep you another day just to be sure. You should get up and try to move around," the doctor said, as he arose and began scribbling some notes on a clipboard. "Just take it easy, walk slowly around the hall with your wife. Don't try to do too much. You'll discover you're still a little woozy and weak."

He flashed a movie star smile at Brenda. "We're so glad you're going to be alright Alex. If things continue to progress, I don't see why you can't leave the hospital Friday."

"What about flying back to San Francisco?" I asked.

"Let's talk about that tomorrow. It's simply a matter of how comfortable you'll be sitting on an airplane flight."

I nodded.

"I'll check on you later. Mrs. Hurley, let me know if you need anything—anything at all. We will continue to monitor Mr. Hurley. If there's any sign of a fever, that could delay your release. In the meantime, I'll see if we can rustle up some breakfast for your husband."

"That's great news, Alex," Brenda said with a smile. "And you get breakfast."

"Now, if I just had a typewriter, I could go back to work."

"Down boy! Just take it easy. After you eat, let's try to take a walk and see how that goes."

Breakfast arrived in the form of something yellow, which was once an egg, and some toast that tasted like cardboard. At least there was a couple pieces of bacon.

While I munched on my first solid food, Brenda and I watched the news and the raw video of the chaos in the pantry following the shooting.

Next, we saw a live shot of a hearse transporting Bobby's body to the airport to fly him back to New York. I saw Coretta Scott King and Jackie Kennedy getting on the plane with Ethel who was shrouded in black. It was so reminiscent of the news film of JFK's body being loaded onto the plane in Dallas.

In the foreground of the sad scene, Sander Vanocur of NBC News said the sight of the three widows was a grim reminder that in America "somehow, some way, we seem to be sending a great many of our young leaders to early graves."

Later in the day, since I couldn't get to the newsroom, the newsroom came to me.

5

EYEWITNESS

"Few will have the greatness to bend history itself; but each of us can work to change a small portion of events, and in the total of all those acts will be written the history of this generation." – Robert F. Kennedy

Despite my bravado, my first challenge was to try to walk. My feet had not been on the ground since I was gunned down.

The nurse removed the IV from my arm and various other tubes holding me prisoner. I sat on the edge of the bed, collecting myself, and I fastened on a hospital robe. An anxious looking Brenda waited to escort me.

"Take it easy. Don't overdo it. Just nice and slow," she said, extending her arm. I smiled at her and slid off the edge of the bed. My legs felt as wobbly as a newborn colt.

The nurse lingered nearby and nodded. "If you feel dizzy, just stop."

I held onto Brenda's arm and began walking slowly down the hall. We didn't say much, just concentrated on the task at hand. It felt good to move again. I was motivated to successfully complete this task, since it was a prerequisite to busting out of this place.

As we entered the hall, it was obvious where Senator Kennedy had been. I saw the two "fierce" looking sentinels Brenda had encountered. I wondered what they were guarding.

We soon ran out of hallway and turned to go back. I felt like I'd had enough anyway. As Brenda and I came around the corner and headed for my room, I could see my boss Phil, John Greer, and a tall woman with red hair, who I'd never seen before, hauling items into my room.

"I wonder what they're doing," I said under my breath. "I've always thought Phil looks like Larry Tate *Bewitched*. You know—Darin Stephens' boss."

Brenda chuckled, but she was concentrating on making sure I stayed upright.

Phil had thick curly white hair and a mustache, and I privately thought he wasn't nearly as charming as he imagined. However, to give Phil his due, he had over 20 years of experience under his belt and spent time in Washington D.C. covering Capitol Hill.

As we entered the room, I was greeted warmly, and everyone seemed glad to see me walking again. I groaned as Brenda helped me ease into a chair. "That walk kicked my butt. I seem to have no energy."

"It's gonna take some time for him to heal," Brenda cautioned.

John reached into his camera bag and retrieved something for me. It was my reporter's notepad that I had used since I began covering Bobby's campaign in Oregon. The outside of the notebook was covered with dried blood.

"Thanks, man. I wondered what happened to it. It means a lot to me—especially now."

The woman who accompanied Phil and John into the room set up a portable typewriter on a small table. She rose to greet me with an outstretched hand. "I'm Lisa O'Dowd. I've heard a lot about you."

"I can only imagine," I joked.

She smiled. "I start working for the *Associated Press* in your office in about a week. I'm getting ready to move to San Francisco. I've been working for the *United Press International*'s Los Angeles Bureau. Mr. Cochran is borrowing me to help get your story out."

"Welcome aboard. Don't call him Mr. Cochran," I teased. "He already has an overinflated view of himself."

"Lisa's respectful. She's not a wiseass like you and your compadre here," Phil countered.

John extended his arms. "What did *I* do?"

I looked Lisa over . She looked very professional and fresh as a daisy with white, pale skin and large green eyes, and her shoulder-length red hair was pulled back in a ponytail. She was wearing a black dress with white nylons, giving her a clean, crisp look.

As I settled into my chair and tried to get comfortable, Brenda brought me some water.

Phil turned serious. "How ya doing, buddy boy?"

"I thought I was doing pretty well, but my walk down the hall took it out of me." I shook my head.

"You up to this? We can give you a little time," Phil asked.

"I'm confused. What are we doing?"

Phil tried to help me refocus. "Lisa's going to take your story—your eyewitness account of the shooting. Ready?"

I shot a glance at Brenda who looked concerned. I could tell she had her doubts but remained mum. I broke the silence.

"I'll type it up. Lisa doesn't need..."

"No, Alex—don't be ridiculous," Phil interrupted. "Just dictate it to Lisa. Think of it like you're in a phone booth in LA calling in a story, and Lisa is in San Francisco answering the phone and typing."

Lisa said nothing but held her hands poised over the keyboard and smiled politely.

"What's wrong?" Brenda asked.

I flexed my hand, which was still heavily wrapped in an ace bandage. "I guess you're right—my hand's still not one hundred percent..."

"More like 30%," Phil remarked,

"I was sure worried about you, mate," John said. "After you went down, I kept trying to get people away from you. Everyone was surging forward to see Senator Kennedy, and no one paid any attention to you on the ground in a pool of blood. I didn't know how badly you were hurt, but with all the blood it looked bad—really bad."

The room was quiet for a moment. I was lost in my thoughts of this horrible nightmare, playing itself out right in front of us. I realized all eyes were on me waiting for me to begin.

Phil tried to jump start the process. "Before we start, John, snap some pictures of Alex here in his hospital room. Maybe get Brenda in some of the pictures."

Brenda quickly recoiled. "No, no! No pictures of me."

John nodded. I looked at Brenda with a pained expression. She quickly pulled a comb and a compact out of her purse. For the first time, I got a good look at myself. "Oh no!" I exclaimed. My longish hair looked like it had been combed with an egg beater, and my face looked pale and bruised.

Brenda swooped in and ran the comb through my hair. "Just a sec," she said as she went into the bathroom and got the comb wet. As she combed my hair, I discovered a painful knot on my head, probably from falling into the wall when I collapsed.

"There," she proclaimed, "that looks better." She quickly retreated across the room and stood behind Lisa well out of the range of John's camera.

Lisa sat at the keyboard but put her hands in her lap. "Begin when you're ready, but there's no hurry."

I nodded. After a few moments of collecting my thoughts, I began.

"Robert Kennedy's presidential campaign rolled into Los Angeles, facing a do or die situation…"

The keys of the typewriter began clicking, then I halted my narrative.

"Wait stop. I'm sorry. I can't say 'do or die.' Let me start again…" I closed my eyes and sighed.

"No problem, Alex," Lisa said softly. She crumpled the paper and loaded a fresh sheet into the typewriter.

EXCLUSIVE REPORT
BY ALEXANDER HURLEY
@Copyright The Association Press

LOS ANGELES — Senator Robert F. Kennedy won a resounding victory in the critical California primary, besting Senator Eugene McCarthy, 48 percent to 42 percent. The count had been unusually slow on election night, due to some new voting machines in Los Angeles. However, four hours after the polls closed, Senator Kennedy was ready to declare victory.

After Senator Kennedy's victory speech just after midnight, I was just a few feet away from him when the first shot was fired. I had been following him and Rosey Grier as they left the podium and pushed through the crowd to leave the ballroom at the Ambassador Hotel.

Ironically, I was trying to keep an eye on the back of Senator Kennedy's head.

The enormous, rowdy crowd at the hotel was singing and dancing with their white straw hats, balloons and various banners with slogans like "Kennedy '68" or "Sock It to 'Em, Bobby" created a festive atmosphere.

The overwhelming memory I have of the ballroom that night was it was so hot—stifling.

It was wall-to-wall people packed into the room, and more and more people kept coming. When word got out that Bobby was coming down to make a victory speech, another wave of people pushed their way into the chaotic ballroom.

When Senator Kennedy and his wife Ethel initially entered, there had been wild cheering and a celebration. The crowd began to surge towards the podium, jostling me. I was struggling to keep my feet, while taking notes as Senator Kennedy spoke.

The crush of the crowd actually pushed me to the edge of the makeshift stage, and I was looking almost straight up at Senator Kennedy's face as he spoke.

RFK said, among other things, "What I think is quite clear is that we can work together in the last analysis. The country wants to move in another direction, and we want peace in Vietnam." The peace in Vietnam line elicited a huge roar from the crowd.

There were colored balloons floating around the ballroom. I will never feel the same about balloons. At one point, a blue balloon hovered in the air, blocking my view of Senator Kennedy during the speech.

The balloons kept popping. After being in Vietnam, any sudden popping sound—especially behind me—startles me. No one who traveled with the Kennedy campaign liked popping sounds. It unnerved everyone. It was an unspoken fear we all shared. Now balloons were scattered all over the hotel, and random pops were heard everywhere.

When Senator Kennedy concluded his speech, he flashed the peace symbol and uttered the now infamous words "Now it's onto Chicago, and let's win there." A thunderous cheer erupted from the crowd.

We had been told before the speech that Senator Kennedy would walk through the ballroom to greet supporters and head for the elevators.

Then there was a last-minute change. I'm unclear why plans changed, but after days of being roughed up by huge crowds, perhaps Senator Kennedy was just weary.

We had pressured the campaign for another press conference so we could get more information in time for the deadlines for the morning papers. It was already after midnight, and there wasn't much time to get our stories filed.

The Kennedy entourage headed away from the crowd in the ballroom through a swinging door into the kitchen. I asked a campaign staffer where we were going, and he said we were walking through the kitchen to get to the press area in the Colonial Room behind the ballroom where the senator would take some questions. My colleague, photographer John Greer, and I pushed our way towards the kitchen.

I had learned at numerous Kennedy rallies to keep an eye on the very large, All-Pro football star, and Kennedy bodyguard, Roosevelt Grier. He was always the largest person in the crowd, and Senator Kennedy was never more than an arm's length away from him.

As we left the ballroom, we didn't know Sirhan Sirhan was waiting…

"Just a sec," Lisa said as she quickly rolled another piece of paper into the typewriter. "Okay, go ahead."

"What were my last words?" I asked.

"As we left the ballroom, we didn't know Sirhan Sirhan was waiting."

I nodded and continued…

As we left the ballroom, we didn't know Sirhan Sirhan was waiting… I'm told behind a rack of trays. I never really saw him. As I watched Senator Kennedy, I saw him suddenly spin around and fall. It confused me, but only for a second. I lost sight of RFK, but I could still see Rosey when I heard a rapid series of pops. It was distinctly different than the sound of popping balloons. It was clearly small caliber gunfire. I heard all the screaming and shouting, and I saw Rosey and bodyguard and Olympian Rafer Johnson wrestling with someone. I got pushed hard into the cinder block wall of the corridor.

It was then that I felt an odd sensation of wetness and a sharp pain in my side. I reached under my blue blazer and saw the blood. It covered my hand. I involuntarily sank onto the floor. It was a strange moment. I thought I was going to die.

I felt I was drifting in and out of consciousness. The screaming, yelling, and jostling got worse. I was just a few feet away from the wounded senator. I briefly caught a glimpse of Ethel rushing towards Bobby.

As the crowd pressed forward to help Senator Kennedy, I was trampled. I had a gunshot wound just above my belt line in my side. Additionally, my hand was walked on several times, as was my left leg. My doctor says I have a severely sprained knee and possibly broken bones in my hand.

I remember being put into the ambulance, and the next thing I remember was waking up after surgery in a room just down the hall from Senator Kennedy's room in Good Samaritan Hospital.

I will make a full recovery. However, I can only hope the same for our nation.

When we arrived in Los Angeles, I got my last chance to interview Senator Kennedy.

The clattering of the typewriter keys halted. I stopped the narrative and tried to discreetly brush some tears from my eyes. I opened my bloody notepad and flipped through it.

"Is there more?" Lisa asked.

I nodded. "Just give me a minute."

"Sure. There's no hurry," Lisa said quietly, as our eyes met for the first time.

"Okay. Start again."

The weather in Los Angeles turned gray and gloomy on Tuesday, but inside the Ambassador Hotel, it was electric in anticipation of a good night. After the disappointment of the upset loss in the Oregon primary, everyone in the Kennedy camp was expecting a big win.

I asked Senator Kennedy, "What happens now?" Meaning, if he won the California primary, which it looked like he would, where would he go from there?

Senator Kennedy said that he would fly back to New York tomorrow for some meetings. He planned to go to Niagara Falls and then motorcade to Buffalo for some rallies. Then he would be meeting with supporters to Vice President Hubert Humphrey to see if he can get them to switch their votes.

After that, he planned to travel to the other primary states and hopefully win there to get ready for the Chicago convention.

"We'll have to struggle," he said, "but I don't want to get too far ahead of myself. We need to win tonight."

A reliable source in the campaign had told me on Tuesday that there had been discussions about trying to gain McCarthy's support. I was told they might offer a Secretary of State job to McCarthy in exchange for his delegates.

A win in California coupled with a victory in the South Dakota primary would mean that Kennedy would have won four of the last five contests. In my final interview with him, I asked if Senator Eugene McCarthy lost the California primary, would it be the end of his candidacy?

Senator Kennedy put his head down and replied slyly, "Everyone will have to make their own decisions." I was struck at how exhausted he looked. Senator Kennedy had seemed indefatigable, but finally he was showing the effects of his grueling schedule.

I received a schedule for June 10-24 from the campaign staff. Senator Kennedy's itinerary is now a sad artifact for a life which ended too soon.

I will now spend the rest of my life wondering about all of the what-ifs. I will wonder what the future would have held if Bobby had exited through the ballroom instead of the kitchen pantry? What if the small caliber bullet had entered a few inches to the left or the right and Senator Kennedy could have recovered from his wounds?

At the end of our last interview, RFK broke away from formal interview protocol between a reporter and a politician. He looked me in the eye and smiled mischievously at me. "You asked what happens next... Well, you and I are going to be very busy this summer, Alex."

I'd give anything if that could be true.

I nodded and dictated the old-fashioned newspaper code "30," which indicates that the story was finished. Why "30?" If I ever knew, I've forgotten why. If you ask most newspapermen they will say, "I don't know. It's what we do."

When I looked up from my notepad, there were very somber faces, and Brenda was dabbing tears from her eyes with the back of her hand.

"Great piece of work," Phil declared as they began to pack up their belongings. "We've got to get going. You know about deadlines. A room is waiting for you at the Ambassador Hotel. I've squared things up with them. We've got to head back to San Francisco. You can stay at the Ambassador as long as you want until you are able to fly home. Let me know if you need anything. We'll be talking."

John flashed me a peace symbol as he departed. Lisa walked over and patted me on the shoulder. She flashed a shy smile. "I'm afraid to shake your hand. A very touching story. It's nice to meet you, Alex. I look forward to working with you."

I smiled and nodded. As the trio headed for the door, I stopped Phil.

"Phil, do you have a minute?"

"Sure thing, buddy boy."

John and Lisa left, and Brenda took note of my need for privacy, turning her back to us and moving over to look out the windows.

"What's up?" Phil asked.

"I was just wondering… after the California primary… I mean, was I going to continue to cover the Kennedy campaign, or were you going to turn it over to some of the pros on the East Coast?"

Phil looked confused by the question. "I don't know… I guess it doesn't matter now."

"It does to me."

"You did a great job on the Kennedy campaign. It was noticed. Your coverage of the Oregon and California primaries was first rate. You *are* one of the pros."

I gave him a faint smile and nod.

"You just concentrate on getting better, and we'll look forward to seeing you in San Francisco. Don't worry about your future."

As Phil departed, I noticed Brenda was still staring out the window.

"Are you all right?" I asked.

She shook her head and was blinking back tears. "No. I'm not all right—in fact, I'm pretty damn far from it. I'm so sad about Bobby. What's happening to our country? It makes it so much more intense to be right here."

The room was quiet, with neither of us speaking. She continued her train of thought. "It's upsetting to see you coming back from surgery after being shot. Whoever imagined..." Her voice broke off again.

"I'm so glad you came..."

"Can you imagine me just sitting in San Francisco wondering about you? When someone is shot... well, there's lots of variables. It's hard to know how serious it is. To hear Walter Cronkite say *Associated Press* reporter, Alexander Hurley, was among those wounded in the assassination attempt made my heart stop beating. I've tried to be tough... to support you... but it's all hitting me now. It's overwhelming to be here... to be here when Senator Kennedy died just down the hall. I'll never forget this moment."

"Me neither. I don't know where my life goes from here. I planned to follow Bobby. He joked, 'You and I are going to be busy this summer.' That's no longer the case. I hate the war. LBJ keeps saying there's light at the end of the tunnel. McNamara says we're turning the corner. Without Bobby, there's no light and no tunnel."

We were both quiet, staring into space. I decided to try to change the mood. "I'm ready for that special little treat you brought for me..."

She turned and managed a smile, wiping away tears with the back of her hand and pulling the joint out of her waistband. "Tonight's a good night for two old friends to comfort one another."

6
MEMORIES OF BRENDA

Good Samaritan Hospital - Los Angeles -
Thursday, June 6, 1968 - 8:45 p.m.

"I saw courage both in the Vietnam War and in the struggle to stop it. I learned that patriotism includes protest, not just military service." – John F. Kerry

Dinner arrived in my room in the form of a couple of dry turkey sandwiches. The bread was toasted, but no frills, like mayonnaise, mustard, or cheese, showed up to enhance them.

Brenda inspected the sandwich with a sour look on her face. "Do you think this is what they served the Kennedys?" Brenda said with disdain, only half joking.

Finally after choking down the dry sandwiches, we were alone after the long, sad day.

Brenda and I sat in chairs facing one another by my hospital bed. I was tired of being a prisoner in the bed, despite feeling exhausted and needing sleep.

Tomorrow, I wouldn't have Brenda. She was flying home in the morning, and I wanted to maximize my time with her. I could sleep after she was gone, but for now, I felt myself sinking at the thought of having this unexpected time with her come to an end.

Brenda turned off the overhead light, leaving only the indirect lamps above the bed to illuminate the room. I breathed a sigh of relief. The harsh fluorescent lights in the hospital room seemed to be a subliminal irritant I was scarcely aware of until it was gone.

She lit a cigarette and then put it in a nearby ashtray.

When I signaled to her, she handed me the cigarette, and I took a long drag. I never was a smoker, but I started when I was in Vietnam, where there was an endless supply of cigarettes and drugs, essentially free. Since then, I've only had an occasional cigarette, usually when I was feeling extremely stressed. This moment would qualify.

After taking a puff, I looked it over before handing it back to her. "What is this?"

"It's a Virginia Slim. We've come a long way, baby."

"I didn't know you smoked," I asked.

"Yeah, well… I just started. I know it's stupid, but… I'm going to leave this cigarette burning to help hide the marijuana smell. I don't want our nosy nurse to walk in here and think she's at a Jefferson Airplane concert."

Brenda reached into her purse and pulled out a spray bottle of perfume. She squirted it on her neck and wafted some into the air.

"I love that stuff. It smells like Brenda to me," I said with a smile. "What is it?"

"After all this time, " Brenda lamented as he sat in the chair next to me, "this is the first time you've ever asked. It's called 'White Shoulders.'"

"White Shoulders, huh?"

"I'm going to get more comfortable," Brenda announced. She began to pull off her boots, then reached up under her mini dress and unhooked her nylons from a garter belt. I watched her peel off her nylons and unhook her garter belt to remove it. She efficiently tucked the items into her overnight bag on the floor by her chair. "That's better," she said as she repositioned herself on the chair and folded her legs up under her.

"By the way," I said, "I want to tell you something.'

Brenda cocked her head and waited for my next words.

"You have the most beautiful legs I've ever seen. I would throw in your whole lower body. Your legs are spectacular. I mean that sincerely."

Brenda threw back her head and laughed. "You're hopeless. Thank you, I guess. So I just need a paper bag over my head and bigger tits but I do have some good parts. Have you been analyzing me?"

"*Stop it! Women!* I've spent most of my life analyzing you," I exclaimed, shaking my head. "That's not what I said at all. I'm trying to sincerely compliment you, and you twist it into a criticism of your face and breasts—which are very nice as well."

She giggled and took a drag on her Virginia Slim. "I'm sorry. You're right. Thank you. That's very nice of you." Brenda reached into the waist band of her panties and retrieved the two joints.

"You've kept that in your panties since you came to LA?"

"Mostly." She lit one.

"Lucky little joints," I said quietly. "Do you carry marijuana in your panties as part of your routine now? How is it that when you're throwing things together for a quick trip to LA, you remember to grab your pot? What's your checklist like... Change of underwear? Check! Makeup? Check! Marijuana? Check...?"

"Always with the wise cracks. I'm glad to see your sense of humor is intact." She smiled mischievously. "One for you and one for me. So, here we are. Remember pot always makes me feel amorous, but don't get any ideas. I still love you, in a way, but I wouldn't do that to Tom. He's a sweet, good man. He trusts me, and I trust him. I really love him. He's so good to me."

We both deeply inhaled, and I closed my eyes.

"I'm curious. Is Tom a button-down conservative lawyer? How do you two line up politically?"

"He's a moderate to liberal Democrat. I wouldn't sleep with a Republican. He doesn't like LBJ. Loathes Nixon. He likes McCarthy, but he doesn't think he can be president and has doubts he can end the war in Vietnam."

"He's lookin' better. Good for him. Does he like Reagan or Agnew and all that law and order stuff?"

"Of course not," Brenda said indignantly. "He's pretty close to you and me politically."

I took a final puff on the joint, and I could feel the impact of the drug starting to wash over me. "Who's gonna end the war now that Bobby's gone?" I mused.

"I read in the paper today that 106 Americans in Vietnam were killed on the day Bobby died." Brenda took a drag on the tobacco cigarette before tamping it out. "I heard last week, that a guy I went to high school with was killed in Vietnam. He was going to college at San Francisco State and helping his parents run their dry-cleaning business. He wanted to be an engineer. Smart guy with a bright future. The next thing he knows, he gets a draft notice and is on his way to Vietnam. Now he's dead. For what?"

Brenda and I both stared into the dimly lit room. I was trying to decide if I should tell her a sad story about a death in Vietnam. I hesitated and decided to go ahead. "There was a young woman at the newspaper... younger than you and me... a real straight arrow. She had a boyfriend who was in Vietnam. Just six months ago he was working on a master's degree at UC-Berkeley. The two decided to meet in Hawaii and get married while he was on leave. While she flies to Hawaii, her boyfriend goes on a final patrol in Vietnam, steps on a land mine and was killed. She stayed in Hawaii and waited for his body to come back. We haven't seen her since."

Brenda dabbed her eyes with a tissue from the box by my bed. "Oh, my God! What a terrible time we live in. In two months, we've lost Martin Luther King and now Bobby. What next?"

"I'll tell you what's next. Jay's a Marine. He's in training school at Camp Upshur in Virginia."

"Your little brother Jay?" she asked incredulously. "I still think he's 12 years old! How old is he?"

"He just turned 18. Couldn't wait to volunteer."

"How much did your father have to do with that?"

"Everything."

Brenda's eyes were rimmed with red and she shook her head. "When will he go to Vietnam?"

"Soon—really soon. Jay will be a Marine rifleman. He takes great pride in his marksmanship. That's a very hazardous occupation in Vietnam. Do you know what they do?"

She shook her head.

"They send them traipsing through the jungle and the elephant grass looking for Viet Cong. The way you find the VC is that, without warning, they start shooting at you! You're just bait on the hook."

"Do your parents want that? Does your dad?"

"Oh, yeah. You know how things are in my family. I had a heart-to-heart talk with Jay before I hit the road with the Kennedy campaign. I told him in graphic and agonizing detail what it would be like in Vietnam. I told him war was terrifying—beyond anything he could ever imagine. I begged him to go to college for a couple of years and wait to see what happens with the war. He'd have none of it. In fact, he said he hopes the war doesn't end before he gets there. He says it's his chance to become a man… and please dad."

"Have you talked to your dad about it?"

"As you know, it's hard to describe communication with my father as 'a talk.' He called shortly after my heart-to-heart with Jay and screamed at me for a good ten minutes. He told me to butt out and to quit trying to put crazy notions in my brother's head. Then we lapsed into our usual conflict: I tried to make the point that you can be against the war in Vietnam and still love your country. In fact, I told him that because I do love my country, I didn't want to send any more young men like my brother over there. But you know my dad: 'America—love it or leave it.'"

Brenda put her head in her hands and stared at the floor. "I always liked Jay," she said softly. "He's a cute guy and so much fun. The last time I saw him… he was in a light blue tuxedo and going to his prom."

My head was starting to hurt a little, and I closed my eyes as I spoke. "I hated the war before, but when I went to Vietnam, I saw things there that made me so angry. There's so many stories of young guys I got to know, and now they're gone. I'd see the body bags on the runways at the airport and realize that all of those bags contain broken dreams.

"I really believed Bobby when he said he was going to stop the war. I heard on the radio that last month was the bloodiest month ever in Vietnam for our troops, and if trends continue, 1968 is going to be the worst year ever."

I sighed. "One of the challenges as a journalist is to remain objective. I'm supposed to treat someone I despise, like George Wallace, the same way I treated Bobby Kennedy. I try to be fair, but I'm also a human being. A veteran political reporter advised me when I started covering the campaign to beware of 'charm.'"

"Charm?"

"Yeah, he said to try to keep an arm's length from the Kennedys. He said it's easy to fall under the spell of their 'charm.' Another political reporter, a real pro from the *Washington Post*, said he told his editor he should be taken off the campaign. 'I'm falling in love with the guy,' he confessed. This reporter warned me and some others, 'I think we're (the Kennedy press corp) getting partisan. We're not quite cheerleaders, but we're in danger of it.' He was right.

"Now we're going to get some old white guy as president, who will keep the war going. Humphrey or Nixon will be the next president. Our only chance to end the war was Bobby, and now he's gone... and so is our hope.

"And my brother is walking right into the storm..."

Brenda leaned forward, and I opened my eyes. She searched my face and said, "You need to get into bed. Remember you're still recovering. You've had a big day."

I reluctantly nodded my agreement. I hated for the night to end, because I knew I'd never have a moment like this with Brenda again. "I can't thank you enough for coming to see me."

She said nothing but just kissed me on the cheek. "Let's call it a night."

I carefully measured my next words to Brenda. I didn't want to overreach even though my emotions for her were on full boil. "I want you to know I screwed up. It's all my fault. I really made a mess of things. I should have treated you better. I should have never left... I should have listened to you..."

"Maybe we would have handled things differently now. Let's let it go." She touched my arm tenderly. "I'm just glad you're going to be all right. You're still important to me, or I wouldn't be here. Let me help you into bed."

She was right. I was on the verge of collapse. I climbed into bed. Brenda tucked me in like a child. "When you get back to the city, come and see me sometime. Let me know how you're doing." she said before clicking off the light, plunging the room into darkness.

I heard her undressing and getting under the covers on the couch. My time with Brenda was over.

7

CLEAN BILL OF HEALTH

Good Samaritan Hospital - Los Angeles -
Friday, June 7, 1968 - 5:30 a.m.

"Let's dedicate ourselves to what the ancient Greeks wrote so many years ago, to tame the savageness of man and make gentle the life of this world. Let us dedicate ourselves to that." – Robert F. Kennedy

I startled awake when Brenda touched my face with her hand and whispered, "Goodbye, Alex."

So began one of the most momentous days of my life…

I vainly tried to push up from the tilted hospital bed to say a proper goodbye to Brenda, but I couldn't find her in the pitch blackness of my room. I thought she was beside my bed, but by the time I got my eyes focused, I saw the door open briefly flooding the room with bright light from the hall. I caught a silhouette of Brenda sliding out the door, and then it went black again.

Her goodbye was quick and caught me off guard. I stared into the darkness mulling over things I wished I had said. If only I'd more eloquently expressed how it made me feel to have her come racing to my bedside in Los Angeles to comfort me. I didn't know if she appreciated how empty my life seemed without her. I myself did not understand the void in my life created by not having Brenda, until I had her back for just a little bit, before losing her again.

She's flying home to Tom, now. She's not mine any more. I have no claim on her time or affection, but my life went dark when she left.

It's like in the *Wizard of Oz*. My life was in brilliant technicolor when Brenda was with me, but when she walked out the door, my existence became a black and white movie…

I got an opportunity to go to Vietnam as a reporter early in 1965. I viewed it as the chance of a lifetime, where I could experience and see with my own eyes what was really going on there. I became obsessed with the chance to cover the Vietnam War.

At that time, Brenda had begun working as the office manager at a law firm downtown—the place where she would later meet Tom.

Going to Vietnam had become my fixation, and I talked about it all the time. Brenda was dead set against it from the very start. She was used to me spoiling our plans to go to a movie or dinner with friends, but this would be taking my workaholic behavior to a whole new level.

I cringe when I recall how I would routinely call and tell Brenda I was stuck at the office trying to finish an urgent story before the deadline. Brenda said during one of our fights, "Every story is urgent. Every night is a crisis. Your relationship with me never seems to be a priority."

When the job offer to go to Vietnam came along, she knew there would be no stopping me. The die was cast. The plan to go to Vietnam for nine months or a year was the last straw.

My editor at the time, a man named Mel McPeak, told me that being a war correspondent in Vietnam would take my career to a new level. "It will qualify you for plum assignments in the future," McPeak said. "You'll be rubbing shoulders with guys from the *Washington Post*, *New York Times*, *Life* magazine, and *Time* magazine. In fact, I may lose you to one of them. This will make you a top tier reporter.."

I believed him. I had been told by a veteran reporter many years ago that to succeed you need to go find the stories and not wait for them to come to you. I greatly admired this man and took his advice to heart. When there was a story to follow, I went.

Brenda and I had many nights of conflict as she realized I was going to go to Vietnam, regardless of her reasoning. Finally she stopped talking about it and surrendered. As the time of my departure neared, I remember vividly the night when Brenda told me, with tears running down her cheeks, "I love you, but I won't be here when you come back—if you come back. I can't do this, Alex."

Faced with her ultimatum, I chose to go to Vietnam and tell Brenda goodbye.

Now two years later, I found myself sinking into despair. It had been over 48 hours since the shooting. I felt so alone. Bobby Kennedy was gone. Brenda was gone. I had no idea where my life would go from here.

I had an epiphany; there was no one in my life. Sure, I would go back to San Francisco and work as a reporter, but to what end? I felt completely adrift. My life was an empty vessel.

My doctor interrupted my funk early Friday morning, talking to me like I was an old friend and clicking on the harsh lights.

He didn't give me time to get my bearings before he was poking and jabbing and asking questions I don't ever remember being asked before.

"Urinating okay?"

"Uh, yeah."

"How are your bowel movements?"

The doctor filled the gap created by my unspoken musings. "You've had a bowel movement since the surgery, haven't you?"

"I guess so…"

"You guess so?"

"I've had very little food, but all my plumbing seems to be working."

The doctor didn't seem to be listening to my measured response and had pulled back my hospital gown to inspect the wound site. "It's healing nicely. But take it really easy. Any redness or unusual soreness, have it checked right away. We want to avoid any infection. It looks like you could be discharged today, if you'd like."

My face brightened. "Oh, that's great!"

"Is there someone who can pick you up? I know you're from San Francisco. I assume that's home."

"Uh, yes. I can make arrangements… or something. My boss has a room for me at the Ambassador Hotel where I was staying."

The doctor's countenance fell at the mention of the Ambassador Hotel, and I knew what he was thinking.

Even if I had to ride a taxi to the hotel, I was determined to bust out of this place. I imagined a real bed and real food. Room service at the Ambassador.

"What about flying home? When can I do that?"

"As soon as you are comfortable enough to sit for a couple of hours on a plane. What is it from LAX to San Francisco—an hour?"

I nodded.

"I might suggest first class to give you a little more room."

"So can I leave now?"

"Gee whiz, you're hurting my feelings. Don't you like us?" he said with a chuckle. "Soon. We'll get things ready. Make sure you have the clothes you need. Most of your clothes were ruined the night of the shooting. I'm not sure what your friends or wife brought for you," the doctor said, as he frantically scribbled on the clipboard of papers.

"I'll give you the name of a doctor in San Francisco to see to make sure everything is still healing properly. Make sure you make a follow-up appointment. Let's not get careless. I'll have the pharmacist put together a couple of bottles of pills for you to take with you. After you get those items, you're free to go."

"Thank you, doctor," I said pulling myself up to a sitting position. "Thank you for everything. I feel lucky to be alive."

He actually made eye contact with me for a moment and quit bustling around. "I'm glad you're all right, Alex. You know it could have easily turned out much differently for you and the others. In that confined space, with bullets flying around, anything could have happened."

"And did. Are the others who were shot… are they recovering?" I asked, concernedly.

"Thank heavens, they'll all survive. Not everyone is ready to leave the hospital. I'm really sorry about what you went through. It must have been horrible. Everyone in this hospital is heartbroken that we couldn't save Senator Kennedy."

I looked at the floor and nodded.

"You take care of yourself," he said, with a gently pat my shoulder.

I smiled at him as he quickly went out the door.

I pulled myself up off of the bed to get my bearings. I needed a trip to the bathroom right away, and then I could only hope beyond hope that Phil or John had left me some decent clothes to wear out of here.

As I went to the bathroom, I made the mistake of looking in the mirror. I looked horrible. Brenda had said I looked like Jim Morrison. The image I saw in the mirror was more like Jerry Garcia after a bad three-day acid trip. I hope I didn't look like this around Brenda yesterday.

I heard sounds in my room. It was the nurse who looked like my Aunt Shirley.

"Can I take a shower?" I asked.

She didn't answer, but she reviewed the papers on the clipboard. I expected her to be grumpy, but she gave me a warm smile. "I'll bet you'd love a shower. It looks like you'll be discharged today," she said sweetly. "Go ahead. The towels and soap are in there. Just try not to get your surgical site wet. Hold a towel over the incision to shield it from the water as best you can. I could always give you a sponge bath if you prefer."

I apparently reacted too quickly and too strongly. "No, no! I'll take a shower," I blurted out.

She gave me a sly smile and said, "Very well."

Just then the phone rang. It was my mother. I went through the events leading to the shooting and the aftermath in great detail and tried to answer all of her questions.

"Did you see the article I wrote—my eyewitness account? It went all over the United States and probably all over the world. Was it in the *Chronicle* or the *Tribune*?"

"We saw it in the *Oakland Tribune*. You didn't look very good in that picture," my mother chided.

"I agree. It's hard to look good after you've been shot! They came into my hospital room to take that picture. I had just had surgery, and I didn't even have a chance to look at myself in the mirror." *But thanks for noticing*, I thought.

"Brenda tried to help me get my hair combed for the picture, but..."

My mother pounced at the mention of Brenda's name and interrupted. "How did that go?"

"It went very well. Brenda was wonderful. I don't know what I would have done without her. She was a great moral support. You know, Mom, I was all alone here until Brenda came. It was a very tough, sad time. It's still very sad here. Bobby Kennedy died in the room about 20 feet down the hall."

My mother continued to pursue the Brenda narrative. "I wasn't sure how I felt getting a call from her... I mean, I was glad to hear about you and all, but..."

"Don't trash her. I kept wondering if you might come. She was... she was so kind to come to help me. Her husband was very nice to let her come."

She ignored my shot across the bow about not coming to LA and continued her focus on the Brenda narrative. "He's some kind of lawyer in the city, isn't he?" my mother snarled. She used the same inflection on the word "lawyer" as if Brenda's husband was communist, a hit man for the mafia, or part of a leper colony.

"Yes, he's a lawyer in San Francisco. It was wonderful to see Brenda again."

"Well, this call must be costing a fortune."

"Yeah, plus, I really need to go to the bathroom."

"I'm so glad you're doing better. We'll look forward to seeing you when you come home," my mother said. "Oh, just a minute your dad is telling me something... your dad said that he's glad you're all right, and you need to get a haircut."

"Yeah, thanks. I'll see you soon."

I sat with the phone in my hand, shaking my head. I'm 32 years old and have just been a player in a major historical event that's rocking the nation. All my father can say is "cut your hair." I'd like to think he was kidding. I'm pretty sure he wasn't. My dad never talked with me directly on the phone. He always lurked in the background firing off comments from the cheap seats while listening to us talk.

I entered the shower, and the warm water felt like a healing balm washing over my body. I felt so battered physically and emotionally.

I put my head against the tile wall, closed my eyes, and just let the warm water envelop and soothe me. After the shower, I went to the closet to find what was left of my clothes and personal belongings.

The shirt I wore the night of the shooting was missing. I'm sure it was covered in blood and perhaps cut into pieces by the doctors after I was admitted. My pants were gone too. My blue blazer was hanging on a hook with dark red blood stains on it.

John had brought some clothes from my room at the Ambassador Hotel. There was a UC Berkeley t-shirt that said "Golden Bears" on it, a green pullover sweater, and my worst looking, scuzzy Levis. This is what you get when you send a dirty hippie photographer to get some clothes. No blazers or button-down shirts from that guy. He picked out what he would have been comfortable wearing.

My pants were gone, and I wondered about my wallet and keys… Where are the things that were in my pockets?

I asked the nurse who looked like Aunt Shirley that same question. She opened the drawer of the nightstand.

"We put them in here for safe keeping," she explained.

I thought the "safe keeping thing" was debatable, but I just wanted to get out of here. The nurse handed me a cane. I greeted her with a confused look.

"The doctor said to bring this to you," she explained. "It might help you with walking for a few days until your leg gets stronger."

I frowned at her, but she nodded encouragement. "Try it."

I have to admit that when I gave it a test drive, it helped and made me feel more steady on my feet. I had no sooner accomplished that surprisingly difficult feat when the door popped open and the "Mod Squad" came for a visit.

8

THE MOD SQUAD

"Is everybody all right?" – a mortally wounded Robert Kennedy asked, just after midnight on June 5, 1968

I dubbed the trio of Kennedy campaign volunteers, the "Mod Squad", because they reminded me of the popular television show.

One was a young white guy, with longish hair and love beads, named Mike. The second was a tall slender young black man, with a large Afro, named Nate. The third was a pretty young white coed, with long blonde hair and big blue eyes, named Jennifer. All three were college students from USC and were part of the army of idealistic, young workers who were getting involved in politics for the first time.

They were passionate supporters of Kennedy's campaign and seemed to be a constant presence everywhere I went in Southern California. The last time I saw the "Mod Squad" was when they were celebrating in the ballroom, just before Bobby came down to deliver his victory speech.

When I started calling them "Mod Squad", and they seemed to get a kick out of the nickname.

They saw me slumped in the chair by my hospital bed, they rushed forward to greet me.

Jennifer gave me a gentle hug, gushing, "It's so good to see you up and looking okay. We've been so worried."

"It looks like I can go home today," I announced. I gestured towards some empty chairs. "Please. Sit. I'm so glad to see you guys."

"Home?" Mike asked.

"I'm not going to San Francisco for a few days. I'm going back to the Ambassador Hotel to complete my recovery."

"The Ambassador?" Jennifer asked with a look of alarm. "Do you think it will be hard to go back there?"

I put my head down and nodded. "Yeah, I do."

I then noticed that they were still wearing their Kennedy campaign buttons, holding on to the dream a little longer. However, two of their buttons had a black ribbon attached to them. Nate was wearing a button of RFK's face that had a purple ribbon that read, "We Mourn Our Loss."

"I'm afraid I'd lose it if I went back to the hotel," Mike said solemnly.

"I have those same fears," I replied.

"We just had to see how you were doing, brother," Nate explained. "We all freaked out when we heard you got shot too."

Jennifer burst into tears. "I'm so glad you're all right, Alex. This has been the worst week of my life. It's like when I first wake up in the morning, it takes just a minute to realize this isn't a dream—Bobby's really dead."

"It's a nightmare, but we can't wake up to make it end." Mike embraced her as she cried. "It's terrible. It shouldn't have happened, man."

"I've been wiping tears from my eyes continually since they announced Bobby died," I said. "I kept hoping that somehow…"

"We had hope," Nate spat out, "but our hope died just down the hall here. Now I don't know what will happen to our country. What are we becoming? I'll never forget Bobby comforting people in the black neighborhood in Indianapolis on the night Dr. King was murdered. That was one of greatest moments in history. To me, that shows that with the right leadership, we really can live peacefully together. Picture a world where no one is dying in Vietnam, and white and blacks are living together in peace…" Nate paused for a few seconds and then asked, "Hey, man, where were you when Dr. King was murdered?"

"Oakland. It was terrifying. People were burning cars—smashing storefront windows."

"Damn," Nate said, shaking his head. "It's like Harry Edwards said, 'You tried to kill Dr. King's dream, but now here's a taste of the nightmare.' I can't see a way for us to go on from here…"

"I've been so emotional," Jennifer cried. "Now we're wearing black ribbons. Nate's right on—where do we go from here when there's nowhere to go?"

"I wish I had some wisdom…but I'm kinda of—I don't know—dead inside. I don't feel any hope and I just found out my little brother is headed for Vietnam. He's just 18."

"Aaaah, no!" Nate groaned. "That's a bummer."

There was some silence while the news about Jay settled on everyone.

Nate shook his head. "You know someone told me that after Rosey Grier wrestled the gun away from Sirhan, he collapsed on the floor in the kitchen and cried like a baby."

"I believe it," I said quietly. "I can picture Rosey doing that."

"If you don't mind me asking," Mike queried. "Where were you shot?"

I pointed to just above my belt line near my hip. "Right here."

Jennifer was trying to regain her composure. "So you're going to be all right?"

"Physically. Emotionally? I don't know," I said. "I'd give anything to trade wounds with Bobby. Would you guys do me a favor?"

"Anything," Nate responded.

"Write down your names and phone numbers for me. I want to contact you when I get back to San Francisco and do a story about the aftermath of the assassination."

"Absolutely," Jennifer replied, as she fished pen and paper out of her purse. After writing their information down, she turned to me and said, ""I guess we should get going. Are you going to watch the funeral tomorrow?"

"I wouldn't miss it. You guys take care of yourselves. Don't give up. If you come to San Francisco…"

"Be sure to wear some flowers in your hair…" Jennifer joked through her tears.

"You can do that if you want, but I've got a couch for you to crash on."

I hugged the trio. "I love you, guys. Keep the faith."

"We'll try, man. We'll try," Mike responded. "After all, we are the Mod Squad."

Jennifer flashed a peace sign at me. "Peace and love, Alex."

I looked at them longingly as they rushed out the door, sensing that I'd never see them again. I wondered what the future held for the idealistic trio.

After their departure, I noticed their parting gift on my nightstand. It was a Kennedy campaign button with a black ribbon and a "We Mourn Our Loss" ribbon. It broke my heart.

My life took a stunning turn for the better a few minutes later.

I sat for a while in the chair, leaning on my cane and staring into space, haunted by the memory of those sad young faces. I was startled back to the present when the phone rang. It was Phil.

"How are you feeling today, my friend?"

"Much better than when you were here. They tell me I can bust outta here today."

"That's great news. I got you a plane ticket out of LAX, so you can leave for home Sunday. How's that?"

"That should work. I'm anxious to get out of here. I need to get out of this hospital, out of the Ambassador, and out of LA. Sunday should be about right. I'd like to finish recuperating at home. It's very, very sad here—too sad. I'm not sure I can take it much longer."

Just then a surprise visitor cautiously popped in the door. It was Lisa, the *United Press International* reporter, who would soon be joining our San Francisco office. She came in the door carrying an armload of newspapers.

She hesitated and started to back away when she saw I was on the phone, but I waved her in and said to Phil, "I've gotta go. I have a visitor."

"I'll leave a ticket at the airport for you to pick up, and I'll wire instructions to the Ambassador Hotel. We have a nice room for you there tonight and tomorrow night."

"Sounds great. Hey, thanks, Phil."

My boss signed off with: "If you need more time before taking a plane ride, let me know. It's flexible. You've been through a lot."

When I hung up the phone, Lisa smiled at me. "Sorry to interrupt. I wanted to see how you were doing, and I thought you might like some newspapers."

"Spoken like a true reporter." I brightened. "I'd love them."

She looked around the room. "Is your wife still here?"

"Let's back up. Actually, the woman you met was my ex-wife. I'm divorced. We're not married any more. She's back in San Francisco now with her husband."

"But I thought everyone was introducing her as your wife…"

"Uh, yeah, they were. We never got the chance to explain our relationship in the midst of all the chaos. When she heard about the shooting on TV, she caught a plane to LA to see me."

"That's very sweet," Lisa said. She quickly glanced for a place to sit.

"May I?"

I nodded, and she pulled an empty chair up next to mine. Lisa looked different than I remembered from our brief meeting the other day. Her red hair was loose, and she wore a white linen mini dress and sandals. She was striking.

She extended her arms. "This is normally not my workday attire, but I'm not working today."

"You look way better than me. I'm embarrassed that when I sent John Greer to my hotel room to retrieve some clothes for me, he brought the scraggiest, ugliest stuff in my suitcase. Where's the button-down shirts and decent denim pants?"

Lisa laughed. "John's an interesting guy."

"That's for sure. It's nice of you to think of me. No one was more surprised than me to see my ex-wife, Brenda, standing at my bedside when I got out of surgery. She's married to some highfalutin' lawyer in San Francisco, and they live in Marin County," I explained

"Marin County?"

"It's a ritzy suburb of San Francisco, on the other side of the Golden Gate Bridge."

"Oh, right," she said softly, as she handed me the newspapers. One was the *Los Angeles Times* and the other was the *San Francisco Chronicle* with my eyewitness account on the front page. In the photo of me that accompanied my story, I had wild, crazy hair, and I was lying in my hospital bed—one for the ages to be sure.

But I couldn't take my eyes off of the haunting images of Robert Kennedy lying on the floor of the kitchen. "Who got these photos of Bobby on the floor?"

"Boris Yaro from the *LA Times*. He was in the right place at the right time," Lisa said. "I hear those photos are going to be in *Life* magazine. They are all over the world by now. Those pictures are historical—iconic. We'll see those the rest of our lives whenever someone talks about Senator Kennedy."

"It rips my heart out to see these. That's an amazing photo of Bobby on the floor with the busboy supporting his head. The lighting, the clarity…it's astounding. Even if he got the picture, it could have easily been too dark or out of focus. If you didn't know better, you'd think Bobby and the busboy are the only people there." I studied a second picture—a closeup of Bobby looking and talking to some people hovering over him. "Do you know what he was saying in this picture?"

"Someone in the newsroom said Bobby asked Ethel 'How bad is it?'" Lisa shook her head. "Somebody else told me he was asking if everyone was all right."

"He was always worrying about everyone else," I said, and my voice cracked with emotion. "That's what we all loved about him."

Lisa sadly looked at the newspapers and shook her head. "So, how are you feeling? I was surprised to see you up and dressed and everything."

"I feel reasonably good. I get out of here today. I was talking to Phil when you came in. I have a room at the Ambassador Hotel for a couple of nights."

"How do you feel about going back there?"

"Very apprehensive, but it's better than being here."

"Well, it sounds like you're very busy. Maybe I should get out of your way. I just thought you might like to see the newspapers. I saw this *Chronicle* lying on the desk in the UPI bureau when I stopped by to pick up my things and say goodbye to a few people."

"Goodbye?"

"Yeah, yesterday was my last day. When I saw the *Chronicle* with your story on the front page, I started thinking about you, and I wondered how you were doing. I'm sure you're like me: If I was cooped up in this hospital with all this big news and I couldn't get any newspapers, I'd be going crazy."

"You're right. News junkies can't stand isolation. I *do* want to see the newspapers, but please, don't go," I said gingerly shifting in my chair. "Let me be frank with you: I'm pretty lonely and depressed right now. I could use a friend. Can I take you to lunch? Or more accurately, can you take me to lunch? I'd love to be out in the sunshine a bit and eat some real food. I realize I'm being presumptuous. Do you have some place you need to be? If you do just say so; it's okay."

"I'm in a bit of a transition this weekend myself. I've got all my stuff packed up for San Francisco, and I head out on Monday. But I've got some time. I need advice about where to live… and where not to live."

"I'd be happy to help." I smiled at Lisa just as the nurse returned with pills, instructions, and a wheelchair.

"I won't need a wheelchair. I'm walking pretty good now," I said to the nurse.

"Hon, you could be doing handsprings down the hallway, and you'd still have to ride in the wheelchair. It's a rule."

Lisa jumped in. "I'm picking Alex up in my car. Can I just meet you out front?"

"Yes, on the Wilshire side," the nurse instructed. "We'll meet you there."

As we moved down the hall, I looked at the closed door to the room where Bobby Kennedy died. I looked ahead and eyed Lisa as she walked out ahead of us as the nurse pushed my wheelchair. Lisa was silhouetted against the California sun, which was streaming through the glass doors ahead. It was like I was leaving the gloom and heading for the light—perhaps the light of a new day in my life.

As we went through the hospital doors, it felt so good to be outside. "This is wonderful," I said to the nurse. "Perfect LA weather."

Before the nurse could answer, I saw a Triumph TR-3 sports car pulling up to the curb in the driveway. It was British racing green, and the convertible top was down. To my surprise, it stopped in front of me, and Lisa bounded out of the car to help me get settled into the passenger seat.

The nurse gave me a gentle hug. "Take care of yourself, Alex."

I then turned my attention to Lisa. She was wearing small round sunglasses with rose-tinted lenses—like the ones John Lennon likes to wear.

"I love your car," I remarked.

"Thanks. My dad's a car nut. You can always find him out tinkering in the garage, restoring an old Triumph or MG or Austin Healy. He gave me this TR-3 when I graduated from UCLA."

"I'm pretty sure I'd like your dad—probably a lot."

"What's your pleasure?" she said as she put her sports car in gear.

"Huh?"

"What would you like to eat?"

I thought for a moment. "I think a big, sloppy cheeseburger… and…and fries."

"I know just the place," she said with a smile. "Want some music?"

"I'd love it."

"It doesn't get better than KHJ and the Real Don Steele. As she jetted away from the hospital, she cranked up the volume on the radio and *"For What It's Worth"'* by Buffalo Springfield was playing.

I looked at Lisa with her red hair dancing in the breeze, and then I put my head back on the seat. I looked at the bright, blue sky and the tops of the tall palm trees along Wilshire Boulevard.

I took a deep breath and closed my eyes. I felt like I had been reborn.

9

SIMPLE TWIST OF FATE

Ambassador Hotel - Los Angeles - Friday, June 7, 1968

"I would hope now that the California primary is finished, now that the primary is over, that we can now concentrate on having a dialogue... on what direction we want to go in the United States; what we're going to do in the rural areas of this country; what we're going to do for those who still suffer in the United States from hunger; what we're going to do around the rest of the globe; and whether we're going to continue the policies, which have been so unsuccessful in Vietnam... I think we should move in a different direction... So my thanks to all of you. And now it's on to Chicago and let's win there!" – Robert F. Kennedy's final speech, Los Angeles, 1968

My first bite of cheeseburger was an incredible sensory experience. I suppose I've eaten better cheeseburgers but none more memorable.

I was sitting at an outdoor table at a cool hamburger joint on Wilshire Boulevard on a sparkling summer day with a very interesting woman. I had eaten little food since the night of the assassination, and the subsistence I did have was vile, tasteless hospital food.

Lisa smiled at my orgasmic reaction to the first bite of cheeseburger. The hand-cut fries were a worthy companion to the scrumptious burger.

I chugged half of my large Coca-Cola on ice, and Lisa signaled the waitress for a refill.

"Slow down... We're in no hurry," Lisa joked. "I take it you're pretty thirsty?"

I blushed slightly. "I apologize. I usually don't eat like a wild animal."

"Take a deep breath and try to relax," she said as she delicately sipped her Coke through a straw.

I put down my hamburger, and I suddenly looked around at the street scene. Something was off.

Lisa detected the change. "I didn't mean to ruin your fun. What's wrong?"

"We've just been through horrific events at the hospital, but outside on this city street, everything seems normal. People are walking around, eating in restaurants, cruising around in their cars... It's like the whole shooting and hospital scene was a bad dream that didn't happen."

"I assure you, things aren't normal. There's so much sadness everywhere I go. If you walk into a store or restaurant or something, it's much more subdued than usual. Regardless of political persuasion, people are so sad about Bobby and very worried about what's happening to our country. The war, Martin Luther King, RFK... I keep thinking this year can't get any worse but it does."

I nodded my head and decided to lighten up a bit. "Where do you live?" I asked.

"West Hollywood."

"That must be a gas. I'm very impressed," I said, as I launched another attack on my cheeseburger.

"Don't be. West Hollywood sounds more glamorous than it is. It's nestled between Beverly Hills and Hollywood, but trust me when I say this is not where Steve McQueen and Johnny Carson live. There's a lot of people like me living there. Occasionally you'll see an item in the paper that some Hollywood star, who no one has seen for a while, died in a West Hollywood apartment. If they die in a West Hollywood apartment, that probably means they're down on their luck or taking drugs or something."

"Ah, come on, I imagine it's better than that. You won't stir up much sympathy telling people you live in West Hollywood."

Lisa laughed and looked over the top of her sunglasses at me. "Maybe that's why I look at the world through rose-colored glasses?"

I liked her playful nature. "I did notice that. You look pretty groovy."

"I have to admit I do see celebrities all the time. I went to Ralph's to buy groceries and saw the girl who plays Gidget, Sally Fields, in the checkout line one time."

"*The Flying Nun!*"

"Yeah right!" Lisa giggled. "Then one time I saw Walter Matthau stopped at a red light in his convertible. He waved to me. I also saw that guy—*My Favorite Martian*—ooh what's his name?"

"Ray Walston?"

"Not the Martian—the other guy?"

"Oh, Bill Bixby!"

"Hey, you're good," she said.

"My head's full of useless information."

"You see several others here and there, and I'm sure sometimes I walk right by some movie or TV star and don't even know it."

"What do you do when you see a celebrity?"

"I try to leave them alone. I usually just nod and smile or something like that."

We continued to fill in the details of our backgrounds as we got to know one another. Over the top of her rose-colored glasses, I began to appreciate her pretty green eyes.

She was a Southern California girl, having grown up in San Diego and attended UCLA. Lisa was the eldest of three daughters in the O'Dowd family. She lived in her West Hollywood apartment as a student and just stayed there after graduation when she began working for the *United Press International* Bureau. I was trying to do the math. I'd guess Lisa was 28 or 29.

Then my turn came to talk about my checkered past, my family, and our myriad of issues. I took a deep breath.

"I'm a military brat. My dad is a career, hard-ass Marine. We moved almost every year when I was a kid. Fortunately we landed in the Bay Area and stayed there all through my high school years." I told her I graduated from the University of Oregon in Eugene after growing up in the Bay Area, while my dad worked at the Oakland Army Base.

"Why did you decide to leave California to go to school?"

"That's simple: to get away from my dad."

Lisa said nothing, but she was pensive. It was never fun to tell someone I want to impress about the death march I experienced growing up under the thumb of my tyrannical father, but I continued. "I went to Los Lomas High School in Walnut Creek, about 20 miles east of San Francisco. My mother and father still live there. I have a brother who's much younger than me. He's 18, almost 19, and in Marine basic training in Virginia right now, and he is undoubtedly headed for Vietnam."

"Oh, no. I'm so sorry," Lisa said, putting down her fork. She sensed my angst but listened for more details.

"I'm scared to death for him. I've been there. I know what's ahead for him. My dad made my brother Jay in his own image: a gung-ho military guy. Jay couldn't wait until high school was over so he could join the Army and do his part. He told me it was his turn to serve his country and put his life on the line. I mean, that's all very honorable, but I can't imagine him in Vietnam. Jay wanted to follow in our dad's footsteps. My brother has always had closely cropped hair and polished shoes, and he always answers everyone, 'yes sir,' or 'yes ma'am.' Jay's motivations are pure and idealistic, but I know firsthand what he's in for when he gets to Vietnam."

This tidbit had thrown cold water on our lunch and our light-hearted banter. I tried to switch topics off of my family. "You're making quite a change—leaving LA and coming to San Francisco. If you don't mind me asking, do you have a boyfriend or husband?"

"Never been married," she said displaying her left hand and wiggling her fingers. "I had a pretty serious boyfriend who asked me to marry him, but he wanted me to give up my newspaper career and move to Chicago. He's a finance guy in the stock market and an accountant-type, and he got a new job on the stock exchange. I said 'no' a few months ago; that was in February."

"I hear Chicago's lovely in February," I said sarcastically.

"That's asking a lot of a native Southern Californian. It was a very difficult decision. It broke my heart."

"Chicago's a good newspaper town," I offered.

"But he didn't want me to have a career. As we talked more about what the future would look like if I went to Chicago, I realized he wanted me to become a Chicago housewife and to stop being a journalist. I didn't want to leave California nor the newspaper business. I felt I would have to give up everything I am to be his wife. That was too high a price to pay. That's why I've decided I needed a change of scenery. Plus I've always wanted to live in San Francisco; it's where the action is now."

"I'm sorry things turned out that way but I think you made the right decision." I finished the last sip of my Coke to wash down the final delectable bit of the most wonderful cheeseburger ever. "I'm looking forward to working with you. I really like our AP bureau. I think you will too. Have you always wanted to write—to be a reporter?"

"Like most writers, I've fantasized about writing a book. I mean, not far from my house on Sunset is the Chateau Marmont where Dorothy Parker, Billy Wilder, F. Scott Fitzgerald, and all kinds of others took up residence and wrote books. Screenplays. There's lots of creative vibes around there. I have a fantasy about doing that someday, but for now, it would impossible to make up fictional stories that are more interesting than what we cover every day."

"That's for damn sure. Ah, the Chateau Marmont… if walls could talk…" I mused.

"I pick up lots of Hollywood gossip where I live. Everyone seems to know everything about everybody. I hear Roman Polanski and his wife, Sharon Tate, have moved into Chateau Marmont recently. There's a pretty fast crowd hanging' out there these days. Led Zeppelin has wild parties in their rooms."

"Roman Polanski?"

"Yeah, you know the guy who directed *Rosemary's Baby*. I went to a premiere of that movie in Hollywood a couple of weeks ago—very creepy."

"That's a horror movie, right?"

"Uh, yeah, I'd say so. Mia Farrow is surrounded by real witches and warlocks and gets raped by Satan."

"Really?" I wistfully hunted down the final French fry, which was hiding under a piece of lettuce on my plate. "Sounds like you have a pretty cool life in Tinseltown."

"Well, looks can be deceiving," she said, taking a tissue out of her purse to clean the lenses on her rose-colored glasses. "But back to answering your question: I think I've always wanted to be a writer—report the news. As a little kid, I was fascinated by the newspaper that came to our house every day. I devoured it. I met Dan Rather from CBS at a thing here in LA. I got a chance to ask him why he wanted to be a reporter. I'll never forget his answer. He said, 'Curiosity.' I like that. In one succinct word, that's why I want to work in the newspaper business. I'm really eager to start working in San Francisco."

"It's an exciting time to be a reporter in San Francisco."

Lisa reached in her purse and tossed down a $5 bill. "My treat."

"No way," I protested.

"You buy next time. That guarantees there will be a next time," she retorted, as she tried to distract me in my attempts to prevent a woman from buying me lunch for the first time in my life. "You made reference to being in Vietnam… Did you get drafted?"

"No, no, no… not drafted. I went as a reporter, not a soldier. I was there for almost nine months in 1966. It changed me forever."

Her mouth flew open in surprise. "That's amazing! As a reporter! Like out with the soldiers?"

"Yeah, out with the soldiers," I said quietly. "You briefly met Brenda the other day. She was dead set against me going. It broke up our marriage when I headed to Vietnam. She divorced me while I was there."

"That knocks me out. That's pretty tough stuff."

"I really don't blame her. There was a time in Vietnam when I thought, *This is the end. I'm going to die here.* It was terrifying—the night raids by the Viet Cong, the artillery shelling... Someone made the comment the other day about how crazy it was that I survived nine months in Vietnam and got shot at a hotel in Los Angeles."

"I'm fascinated by this! I don't know how much you want to talk about it, but I'd love to hear your perspectives on Vietnam. Wow, nine months! I bet you have some interesting stories."

"I have a lot to tell."

Lisa leaned back in her chair and closed her eyes basking in the warm sun. I stopped talking and began basking in Lisa at that point. I couldn't take my eyes off of her. We had just met, but there was something about her I found fascinating.

"It sounds like we've both made some sacrifices for our careers," I said breaking the silence. "I have to admit to myself my divorce was my fault. It was like I was unfaithful to my wife, and my mistress was my job. I wasn't a good husband. I was always at the office or out pursuing some story. I'd handle a lot of things differently now. I feel guilty about Brenda, and I'm glad she's happy."

"I'm sure you're being kind of hard of yourself. Your ex-wife must have a pretty high opinion of you to jump on a plane and fly down here after the assassination."

I looked thoughtfully at her and shrugged my shoulders. "I hope you're right."

She grabbed her purse. "Should we go see what awaits you at the Ambassador?'

"Sure."

"Touch Me" by the Doors was playing on Lisa's car radio. We listened in silence. Then the Beatles' *"Within You Without You"* began playing.

"I've missed music. While I've been on the campaign trail, there's not much time or any chance to listen to music like I normally do."

Lisa smiled at me and then turned her attention back to the traffic on Wilshire. "I love music too. I went with some friends and saw the Doors at the Whiskey A-Go-Go. It was out of sight Very trippy."

"I'll bet. I've been to some concerts at the Fillmore. We'll have to go together after you move to San Francisco."

"I'd love to do that. Oh, I haven't told you about the ultimate assignment I got a few years ago. I was sent to cover the Beatles' concert at the Hollywood Bowl!"

"Get the hell outta here! The Beatles!"

"Yep. Complete with a press conference with the Fab Four."

"You interviewed The Beatles?"

"Well, I wouldn't call it an interview; it was a big press conference. The Beatles are pretty packaged and presented in a very controlled environment. It was short but very cool. The concert was madness. I don't mean to be an old fogie, but I went home with a pounding headache after listening to teenaged girls scream for an hour."

"That's still impressive."

"It doesn't compare to hanging around with Bobby Kennedy for two months and becoming part of a historical event. I mean Bobby knew you and called you by name. We do have a lot to talk about," Lisa said as she stopped at a red light. "By the way, we can't forget to have a chat about where I need to live in the Bay Area. I've got a map."

"Let's do that today or tomorrow. I have a plane ticket home on Sunday."

Lisa parked the car in front of the Ambassador and handed my meager belongings to the bellman. I leaned on my cane and slowly hobbled to the front desk while Lisa parked the car. She suddenly reappeared at my side just as I introduced myself to the uniformed guy manning the check-in desk. The hotel employees immediately recognized my name.

"How are you, Mr. Hurley? We're glad to seeing you looking so well. Your newspaper has reserved a nice room for you. If you need anything—anything at all—we are at your service."

I was handed a key to room on the seventh floor. I shot a glance towards the entrance to the ballroom, and Lisa noticed as we slowly made our way to the elevator.

Lisa opened the door to the room, and we were both blown away at what we saw. It was a spacious, beautiful suite with a nice bedroom, a smaller second bedroom, and a large living room with a view of the city.

"Pretty groovy. They take good care of you," she said.

"Believe me when I say this is not the kind of room I had when I checked in here. I've been staying at Ramada Inns and Motel 6s in Southern Oregon and Northern California for two months. Apparently, you have to get shot to get a room this nice."

Lisa snickered at my attempt at black humor.

"Just a question..." Lisa asked, "Is this the suite where the Kennedys were on election night?"

"No, I know that for sure. Their suite was on the fifth floor. I stopped by there on Tuesday night and talked to some people."

"Okay," she said, sounding relieved. "That would be a little too weird if this was their suite."

I decided to tackle the topic that hung heavily in the room. "Let's sit for a minute. I've got a couple of favors to ask. I know I'm being pushy and clumsy, but here goes... I'd like to go down to the ballroom. I'd like to walk through the pantry where the shooting occurred. I would like for you to go with me."

Lisa looked surprised as she sat on the edge of the couch.

"I'll never be here again. If I don't go to the ballroom now, I'll regret it the rest of my life."

Lisa's face flushed, "I'll go down there with you. Are you sure you're up to that?"

"We'll find out."

10

THE PANTRY

Ambassador Hotel - Los Angeles - Friday, June 7, 1968

"What has violence ever accomplished? What has it ever created? No martyr's cause has ever been stilled by an assassin's bullet. No wrongs have ever been righted by riots and civil disorders. A sniper is only a coward, not a hero; and an uncontrolled or uncontrollable mob is only the voice of madness, not the voice of the people." – Robert F. Kennedy

"There's one more favor… If you don't want to or have other plans, don't let me interfere. Tomorrow I plan to watch Bobby's funeral. I'm not sure I can handle doing that alone. It's going to be hard and I'm stranded here. Can you think of a worst place to watch the funeral? I'll come right out with it—could you watch it with me? I'll order room service and let the boss pay for it. We'll get out the maps and talk about places to live in San Francisco, since I'm leaving Sunday."

"I'm planning to watch the funeral too. Sure. You're right. How strange will it be to sit in the Ambassador Hotel and watch the funeral?" she mused rhetorically. "I'd be happy to help any way I can. I'm packed and have said my goodbyes. I'm ready to go."

We walked in silence to the elevator and began our descent to the ballroom. I was sure I was putting Lisa in a bad spot. She had turned quiet and sullen.

During our short elevator ride, I remembered a conversation I'd had earlier. "I interviewed the security chief here at the hotel on the afternoon of the shooting. I wondered how the hotel was going to deal with the huge rowdy crowds that were expected. He told me the Kennedy campaign people made it clear they wanted minimal security presence. There was to be nothing to interfere with the Senator mingling with the people."

"Did they have the same attitude when he was out on the street or at outdoor rallies?" Lisa asked.

"Oh, yeah. Sometimes it was frightening to me. Big crowds would rush his car; there was no security barrier at all. So many 'what ifs.' What if RFK had walked through the ballroom and not the kitchen? It was a small caliber weapon. What if Bobby had a wound like mine or the other people who were shot? What if the bullet had hit him anywhere except where it did?"

Outside the ballroom was a large photo of RFK with black crepe around it. The ballroom had minimal lighting on, and there wasn't a sound. I was surprised to find it unlocked.

When we entered, I looked up and saw some blue and green balloons hugging the ceiling amid the crystal chandeliers. The balloons were all that remained of the giddy, raucous party that was underway just before those awful moments in the kitchen.

Lisa and I approached the door that led to the hallway where Bobby was shot. A security guard quickly materialized. "You can't go back there. It's a crime scene."

I was momentarily stumped, but Lisa took charge. "Sir, this man is a writer for the *Associated Press*. His name is Alex Hurley, and he was wounded when Senator Kennedy was shot. He just got out of the hospital." She flashed her AP press pass at him. "I'm Lisa O'Dowd with the *Associated Press*. I'm doing a story on Mr. Hurley's memories of the shooting. Can we at least look at the hallway? It's really important to my friend here."

The security guard looked around nervously. "Okay, sure, but make it quick. They'll have my head if they knew I let you in. The LAPD and FBI's all over this area. Go ahead and take a look, but please don't disturb anything. No photos allowed."

We nodded. "Thank you, sir," Lisa said to the guard, turning on the charm, "we really appreciate it."

I approached the double swinging door and tentatively pushed it open. We stood in the doorway, looking down the hallway and were quiet—almost reverent, as if we had just entered a cathedral. Our communication downshifted to whispers. There were marks and bloodstains on the floor and police crime scene tape blocking access to several areas. To my surprise, Lisa pulled a small camera out of her purse and began snapping pictures.

We turned slightly to the right into the hallway—just as we did that night—and straight ahead loomed the open door into the pantry. I couldn't help but look at the bloodstains. Some of the blood was Bobby's, and some was mine.

"There's the ice machine and the stacked trays on the right," I whispered pointing in the dim light. "Over there are the steam tables. I remember being on the floor by the steam table."

"There's a lot of blood on the floor there," Lisa commented as she continued to photograph the scene.

"Everyone was stepping over me and on me to climb up on the steam table so they could see what happened to Senator Kennedy."

"Was Sirhan over there by the stacked trays?"

"I've been told that. I never saw him. Ya know, I just had a stray memory flash. Milton Berle was back here that night. I saw him at the party on the 5th floor. So was Rosemary Clooney. I'm not even sure if that's true; it's a weird thing to remember. The last thing I recall hearing was the crowd in ballroom chanting, 'We want Bobby!' We want Bobby!' Then I heard the first shot, and the screaming and yelling started."

"Where were you?" she asked.

"I was probably about ten feet behind Bobby just inside this doorway right about here. I kept getting pushed from behind, but I had nowhere to go. I was trying to follow Bobby and Rosey."

Lisa showed a lot of moxy, walking over by the steam table, taking pictures of the blood on the floor. I was impressed how fearless she was.

I continued my narrative, "After I heard the first shot, Bobby disappeared, and then I fell over there against that wall. I didn't realize I was shot."

Suddenly, I felt panic washing over me. I closed my eyes, and my heart felt like it was going to leap out of my chest. "Please, Lisa... that's it... help me... I've got to get out of here."

"Hang on, Alex." After quickly tucking her camera away, Lisa took my hand, and she led me out. Lisa thanked the security guard again who gave me a side glance and asked, "Are you okay, sir?"

I didn't answer, but Lisa responded for me. "It's very emotional for him. He's pretty traumatized."

Tears streamed down my cheeks, and my legs felt wobbly.

"Would you like to sit down for a moment, sir?" the security guard asked.

Lisa nodded, and he moved a folding chair behind me.

I put my head in my hands and starting taking deep breaths. Lisa gently rubbed the back of my neck in an attempt to comfort me.

She waited for a cue from me. I raised my head, and she noticed my tear-stained face.

"The last few days have seemed unreal to me, but now... now..." I forced the words out between deep breaths. "It's all vividly replaying in my head. I've got to go."

Lisa continued to hold my hand, and I used my cane for support.

We paused in front of Kennedy's portrait outside the ballroom. "We were all so frightened of this."

I felt like I was coming apart emotionally.

"Let's get you back upstairs," she said softly.

I remember very little of our trip back up to the seventh floor, but when I opened the door to my room, I staggered to the couch and collapsed. Lisa sat next to me, put her arm around my shoulders, and looked into my eyes. "You've had two wounds—one is the gunshot and the other is inside. Your mind or spirit has been wounded."

I shook my head, embarrassed by my tears that continued to flow. "This was a bad idea. If you knew me better you would know what an extraordinary thing it is for me to show this much emotion—I mean, to cry. I shouldn't have gone back to that place. I'm sorry. I'm so sorry…"

"Shh… shh… now. In the short time I've known you, you say 'I'm sorry' more than any person I've ever known. There's no reason for you to apologize," she said hugging me, pulling my head down so I could bury my face in her shoulder. I couldn't seem to stop the tears from flowing.

"It's all right, Alex. Just let it out. I felt it too. That hallway to the kitchen pantry… it's an evil place. Terrible things happened there. It's not surprising you're having this reaction."

Lisa continued to hold me and began telling me about a story she wrote. "You could have what they called post traumatic syndrome. I learned about it when I went out to a VA hospital to do a story on men returning from Vietnam. In World War I, they called it being 'shell shocked,' and later it was 'battle fatigue' or 'combat stress reaction.' When someone has gone through a terrifying event, like combat in Vietnam, there can be lasting trauma. This last week has been ghastly. I'd imagine others who were there that night are having the same reaction as you. I sense you're a tough guy, Alex, but you've been through a lot."

I regained my composure and tried to sit up straight. When I awkwardly lifted my head from Lisa's shoulder, I found myself nose to nose with her. We froze, and I looked into her large eyes, which were moist with tears. Lisa was so beautiful and was now tantalizingly close. She broke the standoff by kissing me on the cheek, and then she quickly bounded off the couch. "Let's make a plan about tomorrow."

I remained mum and brushed the remnant of tears away with the back of my hand.

"This isn't a good time to be alone," she added.

"You're right. After Brenda left, it occurred to me how empty my life was. I've pushed everyone away."

Lisa pursed her lips and looked thoughtful. "It's none of my business, but I was wondering why your parents didn't fly down here—like Brenda did. I guess that would have been the natural reaction I would have expected... but like I said, I'm just being snoopy."

"Point taken. It's a long story," I said softly, as I walked over to the bar to grab a Coke. I gestured to Lisa offering her a drink, and she nodded. "A Coke would be great. Wait... is there something stronger? Beer? Or better yet, any mini bottles?"

I smiled at her, and I swapped the Cokes for two beers out of the wet bar refrigerator.

"That's perfect—two beers for me," Lisa joked. "What are you going to drink?"

"By the way, I like your style, Lisa O'Dowd. Snapping pictures and climbing under the police tape."

"I'm not going to let some security guard tell me what I can and can't do."

"So I gathered." I laughed as I carried our drinks back to a nearby table and chairs. I opened the bottles and tried to explain. "In the hospital, Brenda was nice enough to call my mother who asked if she should come down. Things were so crazy, Brenda said she wasn't sure. We didn't know what was going to happen next. I guess that was the end of it. At that point, I didn't know how long I'd be in the hospital or how quickly I'd recover. My parents aren't... they don't... let's just say, they don't understand me and the world I live in. I've always been the different one who they don't get."

Lisa listened, while she chugged her beer.

"I've tried to explain my job to them a hundred times. I've said there are basically two wire services: *United Press International* (UPI) and the *Associated Press* (AP). I work for AP. Then my mother will say, 'So you don't work for a real newspaper?'"

Lisa started cackling.

"Then I say, 'We cover events for newspapers. The newspapers subscribe to our service. For instance, every newspaper can't send a reporter to cover the Giants baseball game, so the AP—someone from my office—goes to Candlestick Park and writes a story about the game. The reporter puts it on the wire, and it prints out on the teletype. The newspapers will pick it up and put it on their sports page.'"

Lisa continued to laugh. "That's actually a very good explanation of how the wire services work."

"Thank you. I thought so, but the more I explain it, the more mysterious my job is to my parents."

Lisa's kept snickering. "So you don't actually work for a real newspaper, right? That's priceless!"

I just shook my head.

Lisa let the discussion about my parents drop and asked, "How are you feeling—I mean, physically?"

"Reasonably well. I can't wait to shed this cane. My leg still hurts. The gunshot wound is tender, but I'm as well as can be expected."

Lisa took a swig of her beer. "We've spoken frankly to one another. Here's my proposal. There's two bedrooms—both of which are bigger than the bedroom in my apartment by the way. What if I swing by my place and pick up some clothes and stay in the other bedroom. That way… well… I don't want you to be alone this weekend."

I gave Lisa a warm smile. "I'd like that. I'd like that very much."

She took my hand and helped me stand. "Are you up to taking a ride?"

11

WEST HOLLYWOOD

Ambassador Hotel - Los Angeles - Friday Night, June 7, 1968

"It is from numberless diverse acts of courage and belief that human history is shaped. Each time a man stands up for an ideal, or acts to improve the lot of others, or strikes out against injustice, he sends forth a tiny ripple of hope, and crossing each other from a million different centers of energy and daring, those ripples build a current that can sweep down the mightiest walls of oppression and resistance." – Robert F. Kennedy - South Africa, 1966

Lisa helped me to a bench outside the front door and retrieved her car. I smiled to myself as the TR3 emerged from the garage with the top down to maximize our enjoyment of a perfect summer night in Los Angeles.

As she drove out on Wilshire, Lisa commented, "It seems so surreal that we're at the Ambassador Hotel. This has got to be the most famous place on Earth right now."

My slow response to her comment caused some concern. She glanced over at me. "Are you sure you want to do this?"

"Oh, yeah, sorry. I definitely need a change of scenery. This is a great idea," I replied over the roar of engine.

"As Lisa accelerated the sports car, she tried to down shift the conversation. "What were you doing before you started covering Senator Kennedy's campaign?"

"I spent a lot of time in Berkeley covering the antiwar protests at Cal and also the stuff going on at San Francisco State. There was a joke going around the newsroom about me. In the past there have been 'war correspondents' like Ernest Hemingway, Ernie Pyle and Edward R. Murrow. I'm called our 'antiwar correspondent' or 'our man in Berkeley.'"

"Even though you went to Vietnam?"

"Yes, strange to go to Vietnam and then come home to the protests. Things really changed while I was away. I've never really told anyone all the things that happened to me there."

Lisa paused. "Maybe you don't want to talk about it, but I have a million questions about Vietnam. Did you ever get hurt? Covering riots is pretty tough stuff..."

"I've been whacked on the head a couple of times by the cops. It's hard to tell what team you're on when the rioting starts. It doesn't help to be standing next to a guy who looks like my photographer. The worst part is the tear gas. It's nondiscriminatory, raining down on the just and unjust."

"What does it feel like to be tear gassed?"

"Like you're inhaling fire into your lungs. You desperately want to breathe, but it's so painful that you try to hold your breath. It's better than being in Vietnam, but your eyes burn so badly that you can't see. I got tear gassed in Berkeley one afternoon and was staggering around looking for a fountain to put my face into. I was blinded, and there were protestors running everywhere with cops pursuing them."

As we entered Westwood, Lisa joked, "You are now on sacred ground. I'm sure you detected the change in the air. We are now on the UCLA campus, and right over there is Pauley Pavilion where the best basketball team on the planet plays."

I laughed. "There's no disputing that claim."

"I always feel tall and gawky, but then one day on campus, I walked beside Lew Alcindor. I felt like a munchkin."

I looked at her long graceful legs as she operated the clutch on her car. "Tall and gawky are not words I would *ever* use to describe you."

She smiled and then announced, "We have now turned on Sunset Boulevard, my friend—more stars than the heavens and some that have fallen from the sky."

"Swimmin' pools, movie stars…" I cracked quoting the line from the *Beverly Hillbillies*..

This launched a discussion of movie stars, and we discovered how much we both love movies. We were still mentioning favorite movies when Lisa suddenly turned into a driveway to her apartment, which was overgrown with vegetation.

"So this is where the Hollywood swingers hang out, huh?" I teased.

Lisa snickered and replied sarcastically, "Yeah, right. This is where the rich and famous live." When she shut off the car, she asked, "Do you want to come in?"

"Sure."

"Don't expect too much."

Each room in her small apartment was filled with boxes—all neatly labeled and numbered. There was a clipboard lying on a box in the living room. It was an inventory of all the boxes with a notation on the side that said either "go" or "stay."

"This is unreal," I exclaimed as I looked over the meticulously formed block letters of the inventory list. "You're the most organized person I've ever seen. Someone got a 'A' in penmanship."

Lisa laughed. "That's what happens when you're raised by two school teachers. Penmanship is next to Godliness."

"I don't mean to rain on your parade, but I don't think all of these boxes will fit in your little sports car."

"Oh, no! Really?" Lisa feigned alarm. "Luckily my mom and dad and a couple of Dad's students are coming up here next week to load up my stuff and truck it up to San Francisco for me."

"Your Dad's students?"

"My mom teaches English Lit in high school, and my dad teaches Political Science and History at San Diego State. The items marked 'Go' will be hauled to San Francisco, and the items marked 'Stay' will go back to San Diego for my two sisters to plunder. I'll be right back," she said, as she disappeared into the bedroom.

She quickly emerged with a small suitcase declaring, "All set!"

I surveyed the boxes. "You're amazing, Lisa. I bet you'll miss this place."

"I've lived here since college. There's some good memories here and some not so good. It's time to move on." Lisa checked her watch. "Would you feel up to watching the sunset on the beach? I know the perfect place."

"Lisa O'Dowd, I'll follow you anywhere."

We drove out to the beach at Santa Monica and walked to a bench, which was the perfect vantage point to witness the end of a tumultuous day. I started the day in total despair, but Lisa stepped into my life and seemed to turn the trajectory of the sad day around.

The lights of the Santa Monica Pier and the Ferris wheel were beginning to take over the night. The neon lights reflected all the hues of the rainbow on the beach sand, which was made luminescent as the pounding surf washed over it.

Simultaneously the orange ball of the sun began to disappear into the horizon painting the backdrop behind the pier a fiery orange and red. It signaled the end of a day I would never forget.

I turned and looked at Lisa and smiled.

"Everything alright? I don't want to push you too hard," she said, putting her arm around my shoulders protectively.

"Everything's fine... more than fine, really. This is just what I needed."

My emotions today had more ups and downs than the Santa Monica roller coaster. Lisa was right. I was in a fragile state. But still...

What was happening? Why was I feeling so drawn to Lisa? It seemed ludicrous to be thinking of her romantically.

Yet I was.

As we headed back to the Ambassador, I felt myself starting to wane physically, but I tried to hide it from Lisa. It occurred to me that I was closing in on a 20-hour day. It seemed like a long time ago when Brenda slipped out to catch an early morning flight and the Mod Squad had stopped for a visit.

When we returned to the Ambassador Hotel, we ordered a late-night dinner from room service.

There are several types of intimacy. As the long day Friday turned into Saturday, Lisa and I were emotionally intimate with one another. We shared our secrets, inner hopes, and fears.

When we finally surrendered to exhaustion some time after 1 a.m. we weren't sure how to end the night. As she prepared to go into her room and I headed to my bed, we stood before one another like chaste high school kids trying to decide if it was acceptable to kiss on the first date.

Then, for the first time, I put my arms around Lisa's tiny waist, drew her close to me, and kissed her passionately. It lasted what seemed like a while. She was so soft, so beautiful…and a great kisser.

12

SO LONG, BOBBY

Ambassador Hotel - Los Angeles - Saturday, June 8, 1968

"My brother need not be idealized, or enlarged in death beyond what he was in life; to be remembered simply as a good and decent man, who saw wrong and tried to right it, saw suffering and tried to heal it, saw war and tried to stop it. Those of us who loved him and who take him to his rest today, pray that what he was to us and what he wished for others will someday come to pass for all the world. As he said many times, in many parts of this nation, to those he touched and who sought to touch him, 'Some men see things as they are and say why. I dream things that never were and say why not.'" – Ted Kennedy's Eulogy at Robert F. Kennedy's funeral

It had been about three days since Robert Kennedy was shot and two days since he died. The experience of mourning his death had been excruciating, while still stranded in the Good Samaritan Hospital and the Ambassador Hotel.

Despite our late night, Lisa and I arose early to catch every minute of Bobby's funeral, which was held in the Eastern time zone in New York City. I was still basking in the afterglow of my incredible day yesterday with Lisa, but nothing could have prepared us for the painful outpouring of raw, soul crushing grief and emotion that would wash over us and the nation as we said our final goodbye to Bobby Kennedy.

I got dressed, walked into the living room, and clicked on the television. Walter Cronkite was on CBS talking about the thousands of people who had stood in line in sweltering heat to walk through St. Patrick's Cathedral to view Bobby's casket.

I still couldn't believe that Bobby was gone and was inside the flag-draped box.

I heard the shower running, and then it stopped. I knew Lisa would appear soon. I was looking over the room service menu when the bathroom door popped open, and through the billowing steam, I saw Lisa blow-drying her hair.

She shot a glance at me out of the corner of her eye, and she knew I was watching her.

Suddenly, Walter Cronkite said something that got my attention. He announced James Earl Ray had been arrested at Heathrow Airport in London. Ray had been on the run for 65 days since the assassination of Martin Luther King, Jr.

Ray was spotted while preparing to board an airplane to fly to Brussels. Scotland Yard officials said that he had been carrying a loaded pistol and two false Canadian passports.

"Hey, Lisa!" I yelled over the sound of the hair dryer. "James Earl Ray was arrested."

Lisa clicked off the hair dryer. "What?"

"James Earl Ray. He was arrested in Europe today."

"Today? How weird is that—on the day of Bobby's funeral."

"What do you want for breakfast?"

"I'll have whatever you're having," she said with a coquettish smile as the hair dryer revved up again.

Soon she came to join me on the couch and gave me a kiss. "Good morning," she said. "You poor man! It was terribly inconsiderate of me to keep you up so late on the day you got out of the hospital."

"I have no complaints," I responded with a smile. I nodded towards the TV as CBS switched to a live shot of the crowd gathering for the funeral. "CBS okay with you?"

"CBS News and Uncle Walter are the gold standard," Lisa cracked. "Let me finish with my hair and you order breakfast. Then, we'll be all ready."

Among those filing into the massive cathedral were President Lyndon B. Johnson and the First Lady, Ladybird; actor Cary Grant; singer and activist Harry Belafonte; the Nixons; Nelson Rockefeller and his wife, Happy; Hubert Humphrey; Barry Goldwater; Kennedy confidant and cabinet member, Dean Rusk; and Bobby Kennedy's chief rival, Eugene McCarthy.

My heart was breaking as I saw Ethel Kennedy in her black shroud entering the cathedral with some of her children trailing behind her. Senator Edward M. Kennedy seemed omnipresent watching over the family and the proceedings.

Jackie Kennedy and Coretta Scott King also sat in the pews under black veils, as a reminder of past tragedies. The mourners listened to Leonard Bernstein conduct a Mahler symphony, and then RFK's close personal friend, Andy Williams, sang Kennedy's favorite anthem, *"The Battle Hymn of the Republic."* We sat transfixed, staring at the television, and when Teddy Kennedy eulogized his brother, he touched our souls.

Tears spilled down our cheeks as we tried to not totally lose it and break into sobs.

Then came a historical moment that no one who witnessed it will ever forget.

Kennedy's coffin was driven to a special funeral train that would transport his body from New York City to Washington and ultimately Arlington National Cemetery.

As the train slowly rolled down the tracks, thousands of people lined the tracks in an outpouring of grief and sadness to catch a glimpse of the flag-draped coffin, which was visible through the windows of the Penn Central passenger car.

Families stood together—brown families, black families, and white families—all of those Bobby vowed to unite. Boy Scouts wearing their uniforms stood at attention and saluted the passing train. So did veterans who wore the hats from their units and held American flags.

Young black teenagers without shirts stood reverently in the staggering heat and some held signs that read: "So Long, Bobby" and "God Bless, Bobby."

Little League baseball players in their uniforms stood like soldiers and waved American flags. Groups of policeman stood together and saluted as the train passed. The massive crowds jammed the railroad platforms, lined rooftops, and some openly wept. The pain and sadness that was reflected in their faces perfectly expressed how Lisa and I were feeling. Blacks, Hispanics, working class whites, cops, veterans… all spontaneously turned out to say goodbye to the man who was their voice.

The funeral train arrived at Washington's Union Station shortly after 9 p.m.—6 p.m. Los Angeles time. A motorcade then took Robert F. Kennedy's body to Arlington National Cemetery for the only night-time burial in the cemetery's history. He was laid to rest near President Kennedy.

After the brief graveside service, lit only by candlelight, I said to Lisa, "I've got to get out of here for a bit. How do you feel?"

"I agree. I need to eat something." We'd been sitting there since breakfast, hardly moving, existing only on caffeine laced soft drinks and booze from the wet bar. "I've never seen anything like this. The emotions are all so raw."

I nodded. "I've got to get out of LA. Lingering at the hospital and now here is smothering me. I don't know what I would have done if you had not been with me."

We took a drive in the hazy, smoggy evening air. It was therapeutic for both of us. Somehow we ended up at a pizza place on Wilshire. We said very little. There was nothing to say. Bobby's funeral drained all the emotion and strength we had left.

As we returned to the Ambassador, a desk clerk called out to me. "Mr. Hurley, we have a telegram for you, sir."

Lisa retrieved the telegram for me to save me unnecessary steps. I imagined the telegram would be from Phil about my travel arrangements.

I was wrong. It was from Jay.

I sat on a couch in the lobby and carefully opened it.

DEAR ALEX,

SORRY I COULDN'T CATCH UP WITH YOU, PAL.

I TRIED SEVERAL PLACES, AND FINALLY MOM SUGGESTED

I SEND THIS TELEGRAM TO THE HOTEL. I HOPE YOU GET IT.

I WANTED TO TALK TO YOU TO SAY GOODBYE.

I'M SHIPPING OUT TO VIETNAM. NOW MY ADVENTURE BEGINS

I'LL WRITE SOON.

I HOPE YOU ARE RECOVERING OK.

LOVE, JAY

Lisa read over my shoulder.

"It's finally happened. Not Vietnam. Please, God, no."

"Oh, Alex…," Lisa said.

"I wish I could have talked to him… one more time… I mean, before he left."

She put her arm around me and kissed my cheek. "Let's go back to the room."

As we rode in the elevator, I took the leap, "If you're up for it, I'm ready to talk about Vietnam. Then you will know why I'm so sad about my little brother going."

She quietly nodded and squeezed my hand

I looked Lisa in the eyes. "I've never told another human being what I'm about to tell you. No one knows what really happened to me in Vietnam. No one."

13

INDOCHINE

Saigon 1966

"**I** grew up in the household of a strictly-by-the-book Marine. My dad generally thought every problem in the world had a military solution. He pounded into me and my brother that when the U.S. military acted, the angels were on our side. The world was full of bad guys. We were the good guys. Always.

"That teaching took lock, stock, and barrel with my brother Jay, but it never took root in me. I went to Vietnam with the bias that our soldiers were the good guys and everyone else was the bad guys. That perception quickly changed with every day I spent with our GIs out in the Vietnamese country side. My heart went out to our soldiers—many who didn't want to be there, but they bravely did their duty. What I'm trying to say is that it was really hard to tell the good guys from the bad guys.

"A wise friend advised me when I got to Vietnam, 'Keep your guard up. Watch yourself, because nothing here is as it seems.' She was right. Every day I spent in Vietnam only validated that warning."

"She?" Lisa asked.

"I met some incredible journalists including an amazing female reporter who covered the war. I thought that some of them would be my friends forever. One seasoned veteran who covered the war and had seen terrible things, told me, 'There's no forever here.

Every surprise is a new horror that you previously could not have imagined.'"

Lisa sat next to me on the couch and tucked her legs up under her. "Just take your time, Alex. I want to hear all about it."

"It's such a beautiful country, but just beneath the veneer is a heartbreaking cruelty. There was a story told by Denby Fawcett, a journalist from Hawaii. She was at the Saigon Zoo and saw group of Vietnamese soldiers standing around a cement pit. Two bears were begging for food on their hind legs. The soldiers threw the bears candy, fruit, and peanuts, and then one of them tossed a lighted cigarette into a bear's mouth. The soldiers laughed as the bear struggled to cough up the burning cigarette."

Lisa had a pained expression on her face and shook her head. "When were you there? I think you told me, but I forget."

"I got to Vietnam in February, shortly after LBJ had decided to resume the bombing of North Vietnam, ending the 37-day pause that had begun on Christmas Eve 1965.

"There was a crackdown by Ky on Buddhist monks when I arrived. I was surprised to see banners carried by protestors in Saigon that said 'Peace' and 'Americans Go Home.'

"I thought we were winning over the 'hearts and minds' of the Vietnamese people.

"At that point, over 2,000 Americans had died, and something like 200,000 of our men were stationed there. I left San Francisco just as it was announced that the draft calls would be increased to 30,000 young men a month. That put into place a dynamic that I witnessed many times that year: enlisted men who wanted to make a name for themselves and draftees who were yanked out of college and just wanted to stay alive.

"There was remarkable access for reporters. We could pretty much tag along when the soldiers were on patrol in the country side, or we could hitch a ride in a helicopter to some faraway place. The first time I wrote a critical article about the military, I thought I would be asked to pack my bags and go home. However, that wasn't the case.

"I first arrived in Saigon and stayed in the old colonial Continental Palace Hotel. My memory of Saigon will always be hot and sticky weather, where you could hardly catch a breath on the crowded streets and sidewalks.

"The emphasis back in the U.S. on the six o'clock news was body count. It was the way of keeping score of who's winning and who's losing. According to the central command, we were always winning. Then, I found out why.

"While I was in Saigon, I began attending what the reporters called the 'five o'clock follies,' where the military briefed us on the state of the war. The longer I was in Vietnam the less credibility I gave to these briefings.

"I made a field trip and witnessed stacks of Vietnamese corpses littering the rice fields. All of these people had been killed by an air strike. The Vietnamese are such small people physically. It was hard to tell if the dead person was a small man or a child. However, I do know many of the dead were old people, women, and children—even babies.

"I got up close and personal with the dead when I began to help the soldiers load the corpses into big nets attached to helicopters. When you would grab some of the dead people's limbs their flesh would come off into your hands—just slide right off the bone. One of the soldiers told me it was a result of the napalm that had been dropped on their village.

"I was later told that Napalm is a jelly-like substance that sticks to the body and then severely burns you, causing excruciating pain.

"The military counted every one of those dead people as enemy combatants who had been killed in the battle.

"I became physically sick when I saw American soldiers take cigarette lighters and set fire to the thatched roof of the "hooches", as they called the Vietnamese huts. I saw our soldiers burn down the home of an elderly couple while they stood by weeping. The couple had very little but now they had nothing. Were they hiding Viet Cong? Who knows? They began yelling things at me in Vietnamese that I couldn't understand, but it changed my outlook of everything."

Lisa and I decided to take a break and freshen our drinks. "Do you want to go to bed?" I asked her.

"No," she replied. "If you're alright, let's keep talking."

I took a drink from a can of Coke and then declared, "It's time I tell you about Margaret Draper. Everyone called her Maggie. She was my friend.

"Maggie was about 5-2, blonde hair, blue eyes, and a very tough, savvy reporter. She worked for Reuters and was based in Paris for a while. She grew up on the East Coast and went to Columbia. Maggie had been in Vietnam for over a year by the time I got there.

"She had to be very careful. It was a tough gig—an attractive, blonde, American woman in a land full of horny soldiers. I never saw Maggie in anything but Army fatigues. She never wore makeup and always had on a baseball style hat to obscure her face and her hair. She scrupulously avoided any romances.

"I was fortunate enough to spend many nights in the hotel bar when Maggie let her hair down—both literally and metaphorically. She was a mentor to me, and I learned so much about the war and the country from her."

Lisa leaned forward in her chair. "How old was she?"

"Thirty something. She was always very cagey about her age," I said with a chuckle as some memories of Maggie's feistiness flashed across my mind. "Sometimes there would be other reporters joining us for drinks while Maggie held court in a Saigon bar, but as time went on, it just became the two of us."

"Was there something going on romantically between you two?" Lisa asked.

"Uh…I'm not really sure how to directly answer that."

"I've got a feeling there's more to the story. What happened with Maggie?"

"I remember the date very well."

"A date?"

"Not that kind of date. I remember it was August 15, 1967. I'll never forget that date because it was the last time I saw her.

Maggie and I were sitting in the bar, talking as usual. She always called me 'Hurley'—never 'Alex' or 'Alexander.' She was planning to leave early in the next morning and head for Con Thien. It was a few kilometers south of the DMZ—the supposed 'demilitarized zone'— (which the soldiers called the 'Dead Marine Zone' because of the constant shelling of the North Vietnamese). Con Thien was called 'the hill of the angels' due to the massive casualties there. All hell broke loose there after I left Vietnam. But on this night, Maggie was determined to get up there and see for herself what was going on. I thought it was an unnecessary risk.

"Uh-oh. How was she getting there?"

"Chopper. I tried to talk her out of going. I even offered to go with her. She said, 'Don't go all soft on me, Hurley. I'm a big girl. I didn't come this far by playing it safe.' Then she said, 'I have to get up before the chickens in the morning. I'd better turn in.' I think she could see the angst on my face. As we headed to our rooms, she called me back."

"Called you back?"

"Then she did something that was very uncharacteristic. She hugged me and said, 'Goodbye, Hurley. Don't worry about me. I've survived worse than this. Tell you what—when I get back, I'll wear one of my sun dresses that I naively packed to come here. I'll wear it for you. If I dress like a girl, will you take me on a date?' 'Absolutely,' I said. Then her parting words were, 'Be careful out there, Alex,' and I said that I would."

I went quiet and put my head down. It was still painful to talk about Maggie.

"What happened to Maggie?"

"Her helicopter went down in the South China Sea near Da Nang. There was a big storm. I was told she was still alive and bobbing in the water after the crash. The rescue team told me they did everything they could to get to her but then she disappeared beneath the waves"

"Did they recover her body?"

I shook my head slowly.

"Oh, Alex. That's incredibly sad. I'm so sorry," Lisa went quiet for a few moments and then asked "Did you love her?"

"No," then I hesitated and admitted, "Yeah, I did. I don't know if she felt that way about me, but I loved her."

"How long after Maggie's death did you stay in Vietnam?" Lisa asked.

"I dunno know—something like three or four months. I lost my drive and determination. You have to be very careful when you are in the combat zone. I became careless, and I think it's because I lost Maggie. I was hoping someone would do me a favor and put me out of my misery."

PART TWO

SAN FRANCISCO

14

L.A. WOMAN

San Francisco - Sunday, June 9, 1968

As we neared the airport, I tried to fix the moment in my memory. I wanted to tuck it away and then pull it out when I needed to remember my unforgettable weekend with Lisa.

It seemed everything was perfect. Lisa, in a blue sleeveless top and white shorts; her rose-colored glasses, shielding her eyes; and her red hair, glistening in the sun, like a bright new copper penny.

Most of all, I wanted to remember how happy we felt, after all the turmoil. Maybe "happy" is the wrong word. Happiness was in short supply that weekend. Maybe I should say we felt very comfortable with one another.

When Lisa took the turnoff for the terminal at LAX and pulled to the curb, I felt a profound sadness come over me. I didn't want to leave her, even though I knew I would see her again in a day or two, as a new phase of our lives began in San Francisco.

She shut off the engine and pushed her sunglasses up on her head. We seemed unsure how to say goodbye.

"I'd like to think I'm not prone to hyperbole and over statement but... regardless of what happens in San Francisco, I will never forget our weekend together, Alex."

"Last night after I went to bed I couldn't stop thinking about you. I took advantage of your kindness. I dumped all my emotional garbage on you. I... I'm not sure what to say..."

"There's no reason to feel bad. We've been going through extraordinary events. I was glad to be able to share all of this—the good and the bad."

I leaned towards her and waited for an encouraging physical sign. I kissed her and said, "It sounds stupid, but I don't want to leave you. I can't wait to see you again."

She looked at me intently. "Alex, this weekend our emotions have been over the moon, but when we get to San Francisco—"

I interrupted her, "I don't know how it will be in San Francisco, but... I do know that I want you in my life. Okay?"

"Okay."

She popped open the driver's side door and bounded to my side of the car. Meanwhile, I pulled my suitcase out of the back seat. Lisa stood in front of me and put her arms around my neck and gave me a long kiss. "See you soon. Get some rest."

"Be safe on your drive tomorrow, and let me know when you get to town."

She nodded, gave me one more quick kiss, and turned to go.

I watched her drive away, negotiating through the crazy logjam of traffic, until she disappeared. I felt panicky—fearful it was all ending and I wouldn't see her again.

I turned and began to lean on my cane and drag my luggage along. I was quickly rescued by a kind airport worker who took pity on me as I hitched a ride on his electric cart. He took off like Mario Andretti, silently whisking me to my gate—a trip that was occasionally punctuated by blasts of his horn, which startled unsuspecting pedestrians, scattering them like frightened sheep.

As I settled into my large, first-class seat, a first-class-looking stewardess, who reminded me of actress Julie Christie, leaned over the empty seat and asked if I'd like a glass of champagne before takeoff.

"I sure would."

I hoped and prayed that no one would sit by me. The last thing I wanted was idle chit-chat.

"So, Mr. Hurley, what brings you to LA?"

"I notice you have a cane. What happened to your leg?"
"How was your week?"
"What did you do in Los Angeles?"
"I was shot by Sirhan Sirhan. How was your week?"

One week ago, I was arriving in Los Angeles preparing for the California primary after covering Bobby's debate with Senator Eugene McCarthy in San Francisco. I thought Senator Kennedy mopped the floor with him. Then I followed Bobby on his final mad dash around California, stopping in San Francisco, various neighborhoods in Los Angeles, Long Beach, and San Diego.

All of that now seemed like a million years ago. In the space of seven days, my whole world was tipped upside down, and I sensed I was no longer the same person who had followed RFK into the kitchen pantry of the Ambassador Hotel.

The airline gods smiled upon me. I was pulled from my deep thoughts by the sound of the doors closing and the engines starting to rev up. I was alone in the row.

Once we were airborne, my thoughts immediately turned to Lisa. I tried to sort out my intense feelings towards her. Life is funny. Just when you think things couldn't get more hopeless and dark, a bright light suddenly appears and leads you in a new direction.

I love to fly into my adopted hometown of San Francisco, especially at night. When I've been away for a while, I feel incredible joy at seeing the gleaming city perched on the hills and spotting the Golden Gate and Bay Bridges.

My most memorable experience came when I flew home from Vietnam. As the plane descended and broke through the clouds, I saw America and, more specifically, San Francisco waiting for me. It brought tears to my eyes.

As my plane taxied to the gate, I hoped my parents didn't screw up my instructions. It would be great if they were there when I deplaned. It would be really nice if we didn't bicker. Wouldn't it be nice if they were glad to see me and had some updated news about Jay?

However, a shocking surprise awaited me a few feet into the terminal. I was blinded by a bright light, and a microphone was shoved in my face by a camera crew from KRON-TV. My bewildered-looking parents tentatively took their place by my side as the reporter said, "Alex Hurley, the San Francisco newspaperman who was wounded when Senator Robert Kennedy was assassinated, returned home today."

There was scattered cheering from a small group of people gathered at the gate.

Reporter: "Welcome home, Alex. I notice you're walking with a cane. How's your recovery going?"

Me: "Uh, I should make a full recovery, but it's been a very sad experience—devastating, really."

Reporter: "Are these your parents?"

Me: "Yes."

Reporter: "How did your parents and friends hear about the shooting?"

Me: "Like everyone else. They heard it on television first thing in the morning."

Reporter: "Welcome home to San Francisco."

Me: "Thank you. It's great to be home."

Reporter: "This is Tom Matthews reporting from SFO."

I handed Dad my suitcase and said, "Let's get out of here."

The bright light was extinguished, and mercifully another cart rescued me and my parents, aiding our quick getaway.

"What the hell was that all about?" my dad snarled.

"Lucky us. We'll be on Channel 4 News tonight," I retorted.

"They can't do that without my permission," my dad snapped, trembling with anger.

"What do you mean?" I asked.

"They can't take my picture and put it on the TV unless I say so," Dad growled gesturing with his index finger.

"The airport's a public place. They can take pictures and talk to us if they want to. They meant no harm. Turn on Channel 4 at eleven o'clock when you get home and see how you look on TV."

My father continued to grumble under his breath, and my mother wanted a complete rehash of all my injuries, walking with the cane, etc. When we got to the car, the conversation turned to Jay, and I told them about the telegram.

My dad was sullen, and my mother seemed very emotional. When we got to my apartment I said, "Please, cut me some slack. I haven't been home for almost six weeks, so I'm not sure what I will find on the other side of my door, okay?"

"We won't stay long. Dad wants to beat the traffic home."

Beat the traffic! I wondered. *It's nine o'clock on a Sunday night!* But I let it go.

There was a mountain of mail against my door that had been dumped through the slot. Everything looked dusty, but the worst discovery was the refrigerator. I'd forgotten about the tray of hors d'oeuvres that some well-meaning RFK campaign worker gave me to take home after the debate.

In my absence, a completely new ecosystem had evolved in my refrigerator. Fortunately there was a couple of cans of Coke and a six pack of beer to soothe my thirst. I would deal with the gore and debauchery in the morning.

I headed for my bed. I turned on the television and awaited the news.

Right on cue, there was a lead-in about the aftermath of the Kennedy assassination. "One of those wounded in the assassination returned home to San Francisco this evening. Tom Matthews was at SFO for the homecoming."

We performed reasonably well, considering the surprise ambush. My mother was smiling and looked happy. My dad looked like a deer frozen in bright headlights on a dark highway.

Suddenly I began to wonder how someone from the television station knew I was arriving on Sunday night. My suspicions immediately turned to my photographer pal, John, who loved dishing the dirt and spreading gossip. I'd imagine John spilled his guts to someone he encountered from Channel 4, and the rest was history. So much for returning home under the radar.

My phone rang. I expected it to be my mother gushing about our family's moment in the sun on the eleven o'clock news or maybe my dad complaining about the invasion of his privacy. Instead, it was a sultry, quiet female voice I immediately recognized.

"Hello."

"You know I took off my clothes and took a long hot shower. Then I put on my nightie, got into bed with a nice glass of wine, and couldn't stop thinking about you."

"Who is this? Sorry, I get these kind of phone calls all the time…"

I heard Lisa's cackle on the other end of the phone. "How's that for a come on?"

"Terrific. Don't stop. Is all that true?"

"Every word. I'm in my bed now—all relaxed from my shower and ready to head out on my adventure tomorrow. I really *can't* stop thinking about you. I turned on the news, and the anchor says, 'There was an emotional homecoming in San Francisco tonight, which was covered by our affiliate KRON in San Francisco…' Suddenly, there is this guy—the one I can't stop thinking about—Alex Hurley. He's everywhere."

"It was on TV in LA?"

"Yep, you're a star, baby. I think I saw your parents, right?"

"Yeah, they met me at the gate."

"You look like your mom. She looks nice. You dad didn't look very… um, happy."

"My dad never seems to be happy. For some reason, he thought I arranged for the camera crew, and then he told me that people can't put his picture on the television unless they get his permission. I had to tell him that wasn't true, which made him mad at me."

"I'm sorry."

"Let's go back to you telling me about you lying in bed thinking about me…"

"You like that, huh?"

"Very much. I've got the same problem. It sounds crazy, but I miss you. I can't wait to see you again."

"Me too. I'm going to leave in the morning. Phil has a room for me at the Hilton down by the Embarcadero—I guess it's not too far from our office."

"That's right. It's just a few blocks away."

"I'll stay there tomorrow night, and then go into the office on Tuesday."

"I'll see you then. Sleep tight. Good night."

15

THE HOMECOMING

San Francisco - Tuesday, June 11, 1968

I was anxious to get back to the office on Tuesday—not because I wanted to put my nose to the grindstone, but because I was desperate to see Lisa.

As far as my work was concerned, I felt burned out. I was going to need some transition time from the events in Los Angeles to jumping back into the fray.

I was trying to evaluate my feelings for Lisa. I'd never felt this way before—even with Brenda. I was so euphoric about Lisa right now that I was afraid. I'd spent a life time trying to keep my protective shell up so I would not be harmed, but now I was so vulnerable—so exposed.

Did I really love Lisa? Or did I love the idea of someone like Lisa? I feared I would be crushed beyond repair if the things we felt in Los Angeles didn't transfer to San Francisco.

About mid-morning I had my briefcase repacked with the items I wanted to take to the office. I tried to decide if today was the day to abandon my cane. I was tired of it.

I walked around my apartment without it and tested my injured limb. I decided I still had a slight limp favoring my injured leg, but the cane's benefits were negligible. I put on some denim pants, my best long sleeve blue shirt, a striped tie, and a sport coat—my favorite uniform for a day at the office.

I knew no one at the bureau had any expectations about what I'd contribute this week. I imagined Phil would be surprised to see me walk in the door, since he anticipated I'd continue to convalesce at home for a time.

I wondered if my poor little 1965 blue Volkswagen Beetle would start after it's long period of inactivity. That assumed it would still be parked on the street where I left it when I headed to the airport to begin my adventure following the Kennedy campaign. My ever-dependable car started right up, and I was off to resume my life.

I had hoped to slip in the door and head to my desk, without anyone noticing, with the exception of Lisa. The office consisted of a large aircraft hangar-size room full of desks for all the reporters. The room was ringed by a series of conference rooms and glassed-in offices for the top management and editors. The conference rooms are essential sometimes, because it's virtually impossible to have a private conversation at your desk.

I walked in the door carrying my old leather briefcase, which had been my companion since I took it to Vietnam, and I heard the familiar sounds of the newsroom—the noisy atmosphere of multiple phone conversations, the thundering sound of a bank of teletypes spewing out wire service reports, and the deafening clattering created by fifty people pounding typewriter keys simultaneously.

But suddenly it went quiet, with the exception of the teletypes. Colleagues began calling my name, and the entire work force rose to their feet and began applauding. I stopped walking, and an overwhelming wave of emotion washed over me.

The applause continued. I put my hand to my chest and shook my head in amazement. I did a visual scan of the room and spotted Lisa standing near Phil's office applauding with a big smile on her face. She looked sensational in a crisp-looking navy blue dress and white nylons. I moved towards her.

I waded through a crowd of well-wishers, who extended their hands, and several women hugged and kissed me. Finally I arrived at Phil's door and smiled at Lisa. I wanted to pounce on her immediately, but we planned to keep our budding romance under wraps at the office.

Phil jumped up on top of a nearby desk and put up his hands to interrupt the raucous greeting I was receiving.

"We are so delighted to have our friend and colleague, Alex Hurley, back with us today. No one would begrudge Alex if he wanted to take another week or two off to recover from his injuries, but he's a tough guy. Alex being Alex—he's back today." There was another round of cheering.

Phil continued, "It's hard to believe that just one week ago today, we suffered a terrible national tragedy when Robert F. Kennedy was assassinated. The dreadful events were made worse for everyone in this room when we turned on the televisions and heard the network news anchors mention Alex's name as one of the victims of Sirhan Sirhan. Welcome back, Alex."

That set off another round of even louder cheering. I wondered what I should say, but I responded at the highest volume I could muster,

"I'm overwhelmed. All of you who know me know I always have a lot of opinions and things to say. But today, I'm speechless. Thank you all. Thanks for your love and concern. It's great to be back home."

As everyone returned to their duties, I turned towards Lisa and Phil. "Welcome to San Francisco, Lisa."

"Thanks, Alex," she said stiffly. "I didn't realize you're like a rock star or something."

I laughed. "Not hardly."

"I disagree. I've been working in newspaper offices for over ten years, and I've never got a standing ovation when I showed up at work," she said with a gleam in her eye.

Phil laughed at Lisa's quip and then asked how I was feeling. He reminded me to take my re-entry cautiously and slowly.

"I plan to just stay a couple of hours, but I was going to see if I could help Lisa find an apartment if she's still planning on doing some house hunting this afternoon."

"I am," Lisa pounced. "I was going to leave after lunch, if that's okay, Phil?"

"Absolutely, we've got to get you situated. That would be a great use of Alex's knowledge of the city, if he's up to it."

"Let me try to remember where my desk is, but just stop by when you're ready, Lisa. We'll make some plans."

She smiled and nodded. "Just a minute," she whispered. Lisa took a Kleenex and wiped smudges of lipstick off of my face. That gesture was noted by Phil who headed back to his office. As Lisa finished the cleanup chores, she flirtatiously flashed her eyes at me but said nothing.

It took a while to get through the throng of well-wishers between me and my desk. Once I got there, some memories came flooding back. I remembered the excitement I felt when I left in May to begin following Bobby's campaign juggernaut to the presidency.

The first items out of my briefcase were the ribbons and campaign buttons from the Mod Squad. It immediately brought back the grim reminder of the realities of the assassination. I painfully pictured the sad faces of the Mod Squad, whose dreams had been crushed.

Just then our receptionist, Penny Wilcox, burst into my work area.

"Oh, Alex!" she said, crying, hugging me, and blathering on about how worried she'd been about me. I knew Penny was sincere, but she was always very demonstrative and emotional…about nearly everything.

Penny told me how devastated she was when she heard Walter Cronkite say my name as one of those wounded by Sirhan Sirhan.

The diminutive Penny buried her face in my chest sobbing, and I stroked the back of her long brown hair, trying to comfort her. At the height of Penny's emotional meltdown at my desk, I looked over her shoulder and saw Lisa standing there, with a slightly bemused look on her face. I tried to break Penny's clench on me.

"Hi, Lisa! Have you met Penny?"

"Yes. We've met," Lisa replied curtly.

Penny barely acknowledged the introduction, but she did pull back. "Oh, I'm so sorry to have lost it, Alex, but I've been so bummed out since the shooting," Penny said, looking at Lisa. "I'll let you two do your work. I just had to greet Alex. Lisa, you'll find that he's one very special man."

"So I'm told," Lisa retorted with a tense smile.

I handed Penny a couple of tissues from a dusty box on my desk, and she retreated, blowing her nose and wiping her eyes.

Lisa sat in the guest chair by my desk. There was a pregnant pause and I waited for Lisa's reaction to all of this.

"I tell you, I had no idea what I was up against falling for you. I've encountered a whole gaggle of dewy-eyed girls, like little Penny Lane there…"

"Penny Wilcox."

"…who've been having heart palpitations all morning saying, 'Do you think Alex will come today?' 'Oh, it will so good to see Alex again.' 'Do you think he's okay?' 'Oh poor, Alex!'"

"You're just messin' with me. That's not true."

"It *is* true!" She gestured towards me. "Little Penny left all of her eye makeup on your clean blue shirt."

Lisa was right. I grabbed a tissue and tried to clean my shirt as I sat down.

"Am I detecting some jealousy?"

She gave me a sultry look. "Could be. I admit I was one of the dewy-eyed girls having an accelerated heart rate in anticipation of Alex coming through the door."

"You know this is going to be harder than I thought."

"Why?"

"To be in the office and not grab you every time you walk by."

Lisa's response was truncated by the sudden appearance of a barely recognizable John Greer. He extended his hands. "What do you think?"

"John? What the hell? I don't see you for a few days, and you go join Sergeant Pepper's Lonely Hearts Club Band!"

Lisa began laughing hysterically at my reference to the Beatles.

"What's with this?" I said pointing to his attire.

John's scroungy unkempt beard had been severely pruned, and his facial hair had been reduced to a long droopy mustache that ended at his jawline. He wore a blue, English seaman's hat over his newly coiffed hair, and he had traded in his horn-rimmed glasses for some round rimless spectacles. He wore a silky looking Nehru style jacket with psychedelic swirls covering it.

"Nice jacket," Lisa quipped. "Very hip."

"Thanks, luv," John said. "I bought it in Berkeley."

"You don't say…" Lisa said, stifling a laugh, as she turned her head away.

"Take off your hat for a second," I said to John as I began touching his hair. "Your hair looks so different. It looks so… so… washed. And your ponytail is gone!"

"Well, here's the full story, mate," John confessed. "I've met this bird who runs a hair styling place."

"A girl," I said, in a sidebar comment to Lisa. "You know… 'a bird.'"

"I got it. Thanks for the translation," she said sarcastically. "I saw *'A Hard Day's Night.'*"

John pushed on. "I met this girl at a 'love-in' in Golden Gate Park. She's very spiritual. She's changed her name to Sunshine Eagle Feather."

"Of course," I cracked. I dared not look at Lisa, because I knew we'd both lose it and collapse onto the floor laughing.

"Interesting name," Lisa remarked. "And she decided to do this because…"

John ignored her question and explained sincerely, "Everyone calls her Sunny. Obviously, that's not her real name."

"Obviously."

"Anyway, I went to this bird's shop a couple of days ago, and she asked me if I'd like to come back after hours and do something really wild and crazy," John explained.

"So let me get this straight: A girl you meet at a 'love-in' says come by after my shop closes and let's do something crazy, but she meant hair styling?" I asked. "I don't have the words to express how disappointed I would have been to find out she just wanted to cut my hair."

My mind was flooded with a tidal wave of wisecracks that I let I go sailing by unheeded.

John ignored my jabs and proudly announced, "I wasn't disappointed at all! I met her after work, and the results speak for themselves."

"Hey, man, she cut off your ponytail! I can't believe it!" I exclaimed. "Your ponytail!"

"Well, it's not like Samson and Delilah, mate," John said defensively. "I really like it."

"But wait... there's something else about your hair that's different," I puzzled.

"Well, she said it needed some highlighting."

"Highlighting! She dyed your hair? You're joking."

"Yeah. Listen I've got to run. More later," John said. "It's groovy to have you back. Peace and love to you both."

I embraced him, but before he scurried away, I asked, "By the way, you don't happen to know how Channel 4 knew the exact moment of my return to San Francisco, do you?"

"Sure, I told them. I wanted you to get a televised 'Welcome home.'"

"Swell."

"I saw Alex's arrival back in San Francisco on the eleven o'clock news in Los Angeles," Lisa added.

"Blimey. On the telly in LA! Well, see it all worked out. You looked great. Well done."

As John hurried out the door, Lisa bent over, burying her face in her hands, laughing hysterically. "That guy's a trip."

"Welcome to San Francisco. Welcome to my life," I commented, but I was still fixating on John's transformation. "I'm sure the secret ingredient in John's metamorphosis is soap and water."

As Lisa continued to laugh, I noticed she had the *Chronicle's* want ads in her hands, with several apartments circled.

"Let's take a look and plan our attack," I said.

"Feel free to weed out any of these, if they're in a bad neighborhood or whatever, and I also don't want to get too far from our office."

I eliminated a couple of them for the reasons she just stated, and then I felt we had a good list to start our apartment hunt.

"Before we go, take a look at this."

I handed one of many pink phone message slips on my desk to Lisa. "This is one of the messages Penny delivered to me when I sat down."

It said, "Please call Mary Sirhan at your earliest convenience."

"Mary Sirhan?" Lisa asked.

"She told Penny that she's Sirhan Sirhan's mother."

"Is that for real?" Lisa asked.

"I don't know. She's called three times."

16

THE APARTMENT

San Francisco - Tuesday, June 11, 1968

I walked Lisa out to the parking lot and announced, "That's my car over there. I can drive you around this time."

"Aw, that's cute, but can a guy who walks with a cane drive a stick shift around the hills of San Francisco? Hey, wait! I just noticed! You're not walking with a cane! That's great."

"I've decided it makes no difference. I'm fine driving. My car's a good car in city traffic, even though it's nowhere near as cool as your car."

We got in and after a couple of kisses, we headed for the first location. I turned on my radio and gave her a quick primer on San Francisco radio stations. "…then there's KFRC, the Big 610." I hit the first button on my radio and *"White Rabbit"* by Jefferson Airplane began playing.

> *"One pill makes you larger,*
> *And one pill makes you small,*
> *And the ones that mother gives you*
> *Don't do anything at all…"*

"Ah, now I feel like I'm really in San Francisco—driving up a steep hill in a VW Beetle listening to 'White Rabbit.'"

We looked at an apartment on Howard Street, and it seemed to be in a rundown building. The second apartment on Kearney Street was nice, but it was on a very steep hill. We decided the steep hill was a deal breaker. The sidewalk was actually a set of stairs, and I suspected the parking would be a daily adventure.

On the third stop, we found what we were looking for, at the corner of Clay and Taylor Streets. It was a neighborhood of pastel-colored, San Francisco-style, Victorian townhouses, nestled between Nob Hill and Chinatown.

The vacant apartment was in a tan townhouse with bump-out bay windows. There was a stairway to walk up from the street to the front door. It had a living room, kitchen, and bathroom downstairs and two bedrooms and a bathroom upstairs. On the ground floor was a small neighborhood grocery store (V-J Grocery)—a big bonus in downtown San Francisco.

A red awning covered the market entry, which was littered with newspaper vending machines. We were delighted to find that down a narrow alley was a garage. It was another rare and unexpected perk, so Lisa could tuck her classic sports car in at night off the street.

The landlord seemed friendly enough. When he asked for references, I said, "Miss O'Dowd is a prominent newspaper reporter from Los Angeles, who's taking a job in San Francisco at the *Associated Press* bureau," as I flashed my press pass. "We're making sure she has a good place to live, and I could line people up around the block who would sing her praises."

The landlord chuckled, and Lisa blushed.

"Prior to coming up here," I continued, "she was covering the California primary and the shooting of Senator Kennedy."

This caused the landlord's face to fall, and he shook his head. "What a terrible thing." Then he snapped his fingers repeatedly, like he was trying to remember something. "Wait a second… wait just a second… Did you say your name was Hurley?"

I nodded.

"Are you Alex Hurley, the San Francisco reporter who was shot during the assassination?"

"Yes, he is," Lisa answered for me.

The landlord started peppering us with questions about the shooting and his observations about politics. That sealed the deal.

"Hey, I've got to show you something," the landlord said. We walked over to the bay window so we could get a good look up and down Taylor Street. "See that gray building on the corner?"

"Yeah," Lisa responded.

"They filmed a new Steve McQueen movie, *Bullitt*, on our corner last spring. This intersection was blocked off with cameras all over the place for what seemed like a long time. Steve McQueen's character lived in that gray building, and he even bought groceries at V-Js downstairs," the landlord proudly told us. "We're lucky to have a grocery store in our building. Hauling your groceries home on our hills is not for the faint-hearted."

"Oh, look!" Lisa exclaimed, looking straight ahead. "There's a great view of the Bay and the Bay Bridge from here."

"Yep. We have an extraordinary view. This is a nice location," the landlord said, extending his hand. "My name's Hal. You'll like it here."

"I think you're right, Hal," Lisa said with a smile. "This is just the kind of place I pictured living in San Francisco—the pastel colored townhouse on a hill. I'm really lucky to have found this place."

"Welcome to San Francisco, Lisa," Hal said. "It was an honor to meet you, Alex, and I'm glad you're recovering from your wounds."

I smiled and nodded. "Say, Hal, when does *Bullitt* hit the theaters?"

"I heard sometime in October," Hal responded.

"There's supposed to be a helluva chase scene between some hot cars," I said. "A souped up Mustang and a Dodge Charger."

"Oh, yeah. The movie people were talking about that. I was BSing with some of the crew down front," Hal explained. "By the way, there's sure a lot of standing around making movies. I guess they blocked off about 40 blocks and ran the cars up and down Portero Hill, Russian Hill and out in Brisbane filming that car chase. It should be something. I can't wait to see what our neighborhood looks like in the film."

Lisa and I had hit the jackpot. It was a great apartment and cool neighborhood. Hal said he wanted to put a fresh coat of paint on the walls and Lisa could occupy it in a week.

We walked around out front and enjoyed the views. We also perused the grocery store and walked down the alley to check out the garage.

"Let's go celebrate," I said. "Are you hungry?"

"Starving," Lisa responded.

"Let's take a drive up in the hills above Berkeley. There's something I want to show you."

I left San Francisco via the Bay Bridge and headed for Oakland. I turned off the freeway, took a windy road up into the Berkeley hills, and stopped at the lookout point, which offered a breathtaking view of the San Francisco skyline, the Bay, and the bridges. Wisps of fog hung like tufts of cotton candy on the Bay and Golden Gate Bridges.

"Oh, Alex, it's… it's amazing…"

"I love to come up here by myself when I need some tranquility. I like watching the fog as it settles on the city. It's magical."

Lisa said nothing, but just took in the awe-inspiring view. She asked a few questions to help her get the lay of the land from our perch on the steep cliff. Below we could identify landmarks in Berkeley and Oakland.

As we stood there, the fog had thickened up over the Bay. "This time of the year, the fog will start rolling in over the Marin hills over there, and then it engulfs the Golden Gate Bridge on its way into the city. It happens really fast sometimes. You know Herb Caen, right?"

"Of course," Lisa replied. "He's the famous columnist for the *Chronicle*."

"He's one of my heroes. I love what he says about the fog. He wrote, 'Newly formed whitish fog, filters through the harp strings of the Golden Gate Bridge, and then puffs out its chest, as though pleased with its dramatic entrance.'"

"You are quite the romantic, aren't you?" Lisa smiled. "What do you like more—Herb Caen or the fog?"

"They're two of my favorite things about San Francisco."

She reached out and took my hand. "I didn't realize you were such a sentimental guy. Do you bring all your girlfriends up here?"

"It's my special place. You are the only woman I've ever brought here," I said before kissing her.

We lingered a while longer, hardly talking. We then drove down into Berkeley to a very psychedelic place with great pizza. It was a great exclamation point on our first day in San Francisco together.

17

FBI SHAKEDOWN

Later that week, I got a chilling visit from two grim looking men in suits, who suddenly appeared at my desk.

"Are you Alexander Hurley?"

"Yes," I said, as they flashed their FBI badges at me.

"Sir, is there a place where we can speak privately?"

"About what?"

"We need a private place. This is a matter that requires some discretion."

I walked into a nearby conference room with the FBI agents in tow and closed the door. All of our conference rooms had frosted glass windows, since most people meeting with reporters, often secretly, don't want to be on display in a clear glass goldfish bowl for all to see. I didn't sit down, because I didn't want them to plan on staying.

One agent was a tall, bald man with horn-rimmed glasses, who looked more friendly than the other burly, thuggish-looking agent, who began the conversation. "We trust you're recovering from the wounds you received on the night Senator Kennedy was murdered."

"Uh, yes, thank you. I'm getting better each day."

"Let's sit down," the friendly agent said. "We have several questions for you."

"And, you are...?"

"I'm Agent Marshall," the friendly one said, and then he gestured towards his partner. "This is Agent Williams."

Williams began, "We'd like to know the exact details of what you saw on the night Senator Kennedy was shot."

"Every detail I can remember was in my eyewitness account a couple of days after the assassination, which ran on the wire service and in several newspapers. I'd be happy to provide you a copy of my story. Remember, I was shot, lying on the floor, and I did not have any kind of perspective to observe what happened."

The two agents exchanged a side glance. Marshall pressed me. "It's been almost two weeks since the shooting. Sometimes those involved in crime scenes can recall other details over time. Has that happened to you?"

"No, I guess not. I don't know what you're asking me. I lost consciousness moments after I was shot. I don't remember being taken out of the kitchen pantry to the hospital. I woke up in the hospital after surgery, and I wasn't sure what had even happened. One of my colleagues had to tell me that Senator Kennedy had been shot... for that matter, they had to tell me that I'd been shot."

"Let's try it this way," Williams said with a growl. "Just before the shooting, you were aware of what was occurring in the kitchen pantry, correct?"

"Well, yes," I said, with a smirk. "Of course."

"Did you see the assassin? Did you see a second man with a gun?"

"A second man? No. I was following Senator Kennedy away from the podium after his speech. I was probably ten to fifteen feet behind him when the shots were fired. I heard the pops."

"What was the sequence of the 'pops' or shots?" Williams asked.

"Sequence?" I paused for a moment to think. "I guess the answer is there was one pop, what seemed like a short pause, and then a rapid succession of pops or shots," I said.

"How many shots did you hear?" Williams pressed.

"I honestly don't know. I think one of the early shots hit me, and it quickly became very chaotic. The crowd went into a frenzy trying to either protect Senator Kennedy or trying to find out what happened. Everyone heard the shots being fired. There's no question about that."

Marshall began making notes. "Did you see anyone else when the shots were fired?"

"Anyone else? The pantry was jammed with people. I don't know what you mean." I wasn't sure where the questions were leading to, but I had an uneasy feeling.

"What was the source of the shots? Was there more than one source?"

"Uh, no… do you mean someone other than Sirhan?" I asked. "I don't know. In fact, I couldn't see who did the shooting. If someone asked me if I saw Sirhan shoot Robert Kennedy, I would have to say, 'No.' I followed Senator Kennedy out of the ballroom. I heard the shots. I saw Senator Kennedy spin around and then disappear from my view. Then I detected moisture on my shirt and realized I was shot. I fell on the floor and was trampled by the crowd. It's just that simple."

"So you didn't see Sirhan Sirhan or anyone else with a gun?" Williams asked.

"No matter how many times you ask me that question the answer will always be no. After I was in the hospital, I saw the video tape of people pinning Sirhan to the ground, trying to get the gun away from him, but I didn't actually see Sirhan in the pantry."

Neither agent talked for what seemed like a long time. Marshall continued to scribble furiously on his notepad, and then he looked up. "Do you have any reason to believe that shooting of Senator Kennedy happened in a manner other than the officially established version?"

I recoiled from them and made a face, shaking my head in frustration. I decided to pop off, which was ill-advised. "Do you mean, did I see someone behind the grassy knoll?"

The smart-alecky reference to the JFK assassination did not amuse the agents.

"A few days after the assassination—" Marshall began, before he was interrupted by Williams.

"It was June 7th to be exact. The day you left the hospital."

Marshall continued, "That's right. So on June 7th, you and a woman, named Lisa O'Dowd, were snooping around the crime scene in the Ambassador Hotel. What were you looking for?"

"Now wait a minute! I completely disagree with the premise of your question. We weren't 'snooping around' the crime scene," I said, rising from my chair. "What are you implying?"

"Take it easy. Just answer the question, sir," Marshall responded.

"First of all, I just wanted to look into the pantry—the scene of the crime—since I remembered so little about what happened. I felt like I needed some kind of closure. Lisa O'Dowd did nothing wrong; she was just helping me."

Williams pounced. "We never said Lisa O'Dowd did anything wrong. What is your relationship to Lisa O'Dowd?"

"That is really none of your business, but she works here at the AP. She's a co-worker. I mean, well, she had just picked me up at the hospital when I was discharged. I told Miss O'Dowd I wanted to go back to the ballroom and look into the hallway, where the shooting occurred."

"Why did you want to revisit the crime scene?"

"It was one of the most traumatic events of my life. I just wanted to see where it happened. I knew I would never be in the Ambassador Hotel again," I tried to explain.

Williams sounded like he was concluding. "Mr. Hurley, if you remember anything else, you need to contact us before putting it in the newspaper."

"I can't do that. That's in improper request. My loyalty is to the *Associated Press* and its readers, not the FBI. Where were you going with this stuff about Senator Kennedy's murder? What are you trying to say?"

"We meant this to be a friendly chat with you, and you seemed very agitated," Williams commented.

I was measuring my words carefully, but before I could speak, Agent Williams changed topics. "You're familiar with several key members of the so-called Black Panther Party in Oakland. Is that correct?"

"What do you mean by 'familiar'?"

"Mr. Hurley, you seem to enjoy playing word games with us and trying to parse everything we say," Agent Williams snarled.

"Look, I'm trying to patiently and precisely answer your questions. You're the ones playing games. Why don't you tell me what this is all about? Is there some reason you suspect me of doing something improper? Maybe I should stop and get my attorney here."

"There's no reason to be hostile, Mr. Hurley," Agent Marshall said, with a disingenuous smile.

"You ask if I am 'familiar' with the Black Panthers. Have I heard of Huey Newton or Eldridge Cleaver or Bobby Seal? Of course I have. I haven't been in a coma. I read the newspapers. I write the newspapers. As a reporter, I covered their trials in Oakland. I've interviewed all three men. Do they come over and hang out at my house, or do we have beers together? Of course not."

"Mr. Hurley, Director Hoover considers the Black Panthers the greatest threat to the internal security of the United States. We take this very seriously," Agent Williams retorted.

"That's Director Hoover's hang-up. We're done here. I need you to leave."

"We also know that you have contacts in the antiwar movement in Berkeley. We'd like to know the identity of the outside agitators in these protests. Who is inciting the violence? You'd be doing a great service to be our man on the inside. You could help us as a source. We could make it worth your while."

"Let me ask you a few questions," I snapped. "Are you watching me? Do you have me under surveillance? And if so, why? How do you know so much about what I've been doing?"

They remained mum and tossed two business cards with phone numbers on the table.

Williams said, "I'll leave you a couple of thoughts to contemplate. You kept asking where we were going with our line of questioning.

Things are not always as they appear to be on the surface. You think you know what's going on, but you really don't, Mr. Hurley. The other advice I would give you is that cooperation is a two-way street. If you help us, your life can become easier."

"...or harder," Agent Marshall, quickly added.

"Let me give you a piece of advice," I fumed. "If you ever want to talk to me again, call our receptionist to get an appointment. I'll have my editor and our attorney here, and it will be a very short conversation. Our little talk is on the record. I plan to make detailed notes. If you harass me again, I'll write a story about this little episode, and I promise you won't like it much."

Williams glared at me. "Good day, Mr. Hurley. We'll be in touch."

18

SECRETS

San Francisco - Thursday, June 13, 1968

I stood in the doorway of the conference room, seething, as I watched the FBI agents leave. I wanted to make sure they didn't linger any longer, and I was hypersensitive to any movements by the G-Men towards Lisa's desk.

She was on the phone, but I knew Lisa detected something was up. She shot a glance at me and then watched the agents walking towards the door. We were like a nervous herd of antelope, looking out the corner of our eye at prowling lions hiding in the tall grass.

I was usually a pretty mellow guy, but when properly provoked, I could feel my genes kick in. Suddenly, I was Mike Hurley's son and ready to fight. My dad never let any slight—merely perceived or real— go unchallenged, which was why he seemed perpetually pissed off at the whole world.

After getting worked over by the FBI, I was trembling with anger, and my heart felt like it was going to jump out of my chest.

I marched up to Penny's desk and said, "If those two guys, or anyone else from the FBI, comes walking in the door, do not let them in the newsroom. I want you to call me or Phil before admitting them, okay?"

"I'm so sorry, Alex. Did I do anything wrong? I thought since they were with the FBI... I mean, they showed me their badges..."

Penny asked with a pained expression, as she appeared to crumble before my eyes.

"No, no, you did nothing wrong. What you did was fine. I'm just saying, next time, let's do it a different way. Got it?"

"Got it."

I then headed to Phil's office. When I entered, he was puffing hard on his freshly lit pipe like a locomotive trying to pick up speed. "Who were the two gorillas in the suits?"

"FBI." I began rehashing my conversation with the agents as precisely as I could.

"I don't understand what they are fishing for," Phil mused. "How many times do you have to tell them that you didn't see the shooting?"

"It gets worse. They started quizzing me about my contacts in the Black Panthers and in the antiwar groups in Berkeley. I told them to go to hell; that it was an improper request. They were playing 'good cop-bad cop' with me and tried to recruit me to be their 'inside man' in those two organizations. I obviously told them that wasn't going to happen."

"Don't talk to them again unless me and Sam Bradford are there to cover your back."

"I used those very words and said, 'If we ever talk again, it will be with my editor and our attorney in the room.'"

"Perfect, buddy boy," Phil responded. He puffed on his pipe thoughtfully and stared into space for a moment. "What's their angle? Did you see a second gunman? What's that all about? This is JFK conspiracy nonsense. Who was the other shooter? Bobby's assassination could not be more straight forward. Eight bullets, all accounted for—where's the mystery?"

"I said to the agents, 'So in other words, you're asking if I saw someone shooting from the grassy knoll'?"

Phil's mouth dropped open. "You did not! You said that to the agents?"

"I did."

Phil threw his head back and let loose with a loud guffaw that could probably be heard all over the newsroom. "That's great—the grassy knoll. By the way, we should tell Penny not to let those clowns into the newsroom unless you or I authorize it."

"I did talk to Penny, but it would be good for you re-emphasize it to her."

We both sat quietly for a few moments, thinking about the strange visit.

Phil broke the silence saying, "They *were* FBI agents, weren't they? I mean, you saw their IDs."

I nodded. I took the two business cards from my shirt pocket and tossed them on the desk.

"There's something very creepy about this whole thing."

Phil looked nervously at his ringing phone and appeared to be ready to end our conversation.

"There's one more thing," I said. "They asked me questions about Lisa."

That caused Phil to ignore the phone. "Lisa?"

"They wanted to know what the two of us were doing 'snooping around the crime scene.' The G-Men knew Lisa and I went back to the scene of the shooting. The only person in the ballroom was a hotel security guard. When I went back into the pantry to see where the shooting occurred, no one went with us. Lisa and I mentioned our names once to the guard. Lisa flashed her press pass and told the guard I was one of those shot during the assassination. I don't think the FBI got the information from him. I wonder if I'm under surveillance or if they're tailing me…"

"But why?"

I shook my head and shrugged, and then I looked nervously in Lisa's direction. She was observing Phil and I deeply involved in conversation.

"You know I'm starting to get some very strange phone calls," I said.

"Like what?"

"A woman keeps calling me and leaving a message. She says she's Sirhan Sirhan's mother and wants to talk to me."

"Is she Sirhan's mother?"

"Maybe—maybe not. I don't know. Usually I'd go after something like that, but I don't want to talk to her. It feels differently when you're part of the story instead of just covering events as an observer."

Phil knocked his pipe on the side of the ashtray. "Your notoriety may be attracting a bunch of crazies."

"I got a call from a guy the other day who wanted to meet me down on the wharf at night. He said he was in the Ambassador Hotel and was there when I was shot. This guy said that as I was lying on the floor, a woman in a polka-dot dress ran out of the pantry and told a campaign worker, 'We shot him.'"

"We? What are you gonna do about that?"

"Nothing. I don't want any part of that kind of stuff. I have no appetite for mystery meetings on the wharf with people I don't know."

I stood up to leave but Phil stopped me.

He got a twinkle in his eye and said, "Hey, sit down for a minute. Now I've got a couple of questions for you…"

"Oh, good… more questions," I quipped. I felt like I'd had enough of being interrogated and wondered what was on Phil's mind.

"Take it easy. Is there something going on with you and Lisa?"

"Something going on? What do you mean?"

Phil threw back his head and laughed. "Who do you think you're dealing with here, buddy boy? I'm getting a non-denial denial."

"Why do you think I have a thing for Lisa?"

"Ah, answering a question with a question—another sign. Why do I think you have the hots for Lisa? Well, let's talk about that. How about when you two are together, the temperature in the room goes up about 10 degrees? She laughs at all your jokes—whether they are funny or not—and her eyes get all twinkly when she sees you.

The way she looked at you when she was cleaning the lipstick off of your face…You, on the other hand, look at her like a hungry wolf."

"Okay, okay, I can't bullshit a bullshitter. I guess we're busted."

"I knew it," he said to himself, pounding his fist on his desk. "How did this happen? When?"

"After you left, she came back to the hospital to see me and asked where my wife was. I told her that Brenda was my ex-wife."

"At first I thought Brenda was your wife too. I thought you…"

"I understand. It was very chaotic, and people made all kinds of assumptions. Brenda decided to let them think she was my wife so could stay in my room with me."

"I see. Boy, I'll tell you, Brenda's a beauty, but back to Lisa."

I nervously laughed, adding, "She spent the weekend with me at the Ambassador before I flew home, and the rest is history."

Phil started cackling. "Spent the weekend with you? So you're telling me I foot the bill for a suite at the Ambassador for your weekend tryst with the lovely Lisa?"

"I wouldn't put it that way, but in a word—yes. But remember I was recovering from a gunshot wound. Lisa was wonderful, very comforting, and we immediately clicked." I got up from my chair and headed for the door but Phil stopped me again.

"You seem anxious to leave. I must have struck a nerve. How much do you know about her background?"

I groaned. "You're not gonna ruin things for me, are you? Please don't tell me she's a Soviet double agent or something awful."

Phil laughed and moved around the desk. We both stood looking at Lisa, who was talking on the phone and typing furiously. "I'm sure her old boss at UPI is still crying in his beer because I stole his golden girl. She was an honor student in high school; an exchange student in France during her junior year; and got a full academic scholarship to UCLA, where she got straight A's. Other schools wanted her too. She also won an award for an investigative piece she did for the student paper (*The Daily Bruin)* and won an award for journalistic excellence from the Southern California

Press Association for a series she did on problems faced by veterans returning from Vietnam. She's gonna be a super star for us."

"Damn," I said quietly. "But I found out she's not perfect."

"How so?"

"She's a Dodger fan."

Phil couldn't resist one final jab. "The only thing that puzzles me is if she's so damn smart, why is she attracted to you?"

I chuckled. "It's a fair question. I worry about that every day."

Phil clapped me on the back, opened his door, and called to Lisa to come into his office. She looked concerned.

Then Phil said the words you never want to hear when you enter your boss's office. "Shut the door and have a seat, Lisa," he said.

"You may have noticed the two guys in suits who came in and went after Alex."

"I didn't. Went after?" she wondered.

"I'll let Alex give you all the gory details, but be careful. If you are contacted by anyone claiming to be FBI agents, don't talk to them. Contact me or Alex, and we'll get our attorney involved. Chances are, Alex will be more accessible to you than me," Phil said, with a small snicker.

Lisa gave me a puzzled side glance.

"I'll leave you two crazy kids to it," Phil said with a smirk, as he pushed the FBI agent's business cards across the desk towards me.

I signaled to Lisa with my head, indicating we should leave. "Let's grab a conference room."

Once inside the conference room, Lisa asked, "What in the hell is going on? I didn't understand a single thing Phil just said."

"First of all, the reason Phil looks like the cat who swallowed the canary is because he thinks he's discovered our secret."

"That didn't take long." Lisa rolled her eyes.

"Phil asked me if there was somethin' going on with us. He caught me off guard, and I said something stupid like, 'What makes you think that?' And then he moved in for the kill. He said that when we're in a room together the temperature rises about ten degrees and I look at you like a hungry wolf."

"Ah, geez, what a rat fink." Lisa smiled and folded her arms. "We thought we were being soooo clever, eh, Mr. Wolf?"

"I guess I'm guilty as charged. I suppose I do look at you like a hungry wolf."

"I'm glad. And I'm just a poor little lamb," Lisa said, with a flirty smile.

"Now about the FBI..."

"I'd rather talk about wolves and lambs, but what's all this FBI business?"

I walked over to the door and said, "First, I need a Lisa fix." I flipped the lock on the conference room door, put my arms around her, and kissed her.

After a few moments, I broke away and smiled. "Okay, now I can concentrate. I could't take it any more. I had to touch you."

I began to recount the conversation with the FBI. I concluded my summary saying, "This is why Phil said that we shouldn't have any more one-on-one conversations with the FBI unless we have him and our attorney present."

"Are you absolutely sure they were with the FBI?" Lisa asked. "Did you get a good look, or did they just flash some badges at you...?"

"I looked at their badges and cards. They were legit. My concern is how they know so much about what I've been doing. Are they watching me? Watching us?"

19

UNSHAKESABLE OBSESSION

San Francisco - Thursday, June 13, 1968

"**W**hat gives! You were a victim of a crime. They're hinting another gunman in the pantry? Then there's the crack at the end about you not really knowing what happened?" I shook my head in bewilderment.

"This is funky. They're trying to intimidate you," Lisa surmised. "Maybe their visit wasn't about the assassination at all. Maybe it was to push you around and recruit you to give them information about the antiwar organizers and the Black Panthers. Isn't Huey Newton's trial sometime this fall?"

"Yeah, he goes on trial in September. That's an interesting thought…" I thought about it, while I fumbled with a folder of notes and wire dispatches.

"What do you have there?" Lisa asked, tapping the folder.

"It's a bunch of stories I've collected that have been coming over the wires. Some from the *Los Angeles Times*, some from Reuters, and some from AP at other locations. Want to hear a creepy quote from Nixon?"

"Is there any other kind?"

"This was after Bobby lost the Oregon primary. Someone asked Nixon for a prediction and he said, 'I think you don't write off Robert Kennedy. He can come off the floor and win in California.'"

"'Come off the floor?' That's weird phrasing. I'm sure he didn't mean it the way it sounds, in light of what happened."

I shuffled the papers until I found what I needed. "There's some background information on Sirhan starting to come out. Do you want to hear it?"

"I guess so. I'm sure it will be upsetting, though," Lisa lamented, as she rested her chin on her fist.

"June 5th, the day of the assassination, was significant to Sirhan Sirhan. It's the anniversary of the Six-Day War, when Israel seized the Sinai, the Golan Heights, and East Jerusalem. Apparently, Bobby Kennedy gave a speech in Oregon, where he said he supported sending 50 Phantom jets to Israel. Sirhan, who is a Christian Palestinian Arab, said, 'I did it (the assassination) for my country.'"

Lisa groaned. "Using that twisted logic, why didn't he go after LBJ or some other current leader. Why Bobby?"

"Sirhan said Bobby *would be* the president."

I took a wire dispatch from the *Washington Post* and placed it in front of Lisa. "This is from papers found in Sirhan's house."

RFK must be

be be disposed of

d d d

disposed of

disposed of openly

Robert Fitzgerald

Kennedy must soon die

die die die die

die die die die die

My determination to

eliminate RFK is becoming

more the more

of an unshakeable

obsession

Lisa sighed. "It all could have all happened a difference way. There are so many 'what-ifs.' Like, what if Bobby had exited through the ballroom as apparently they had originally planned? Would he have ever crossed paths with Sirhan?"

"I've thought about that a hundred times. It's troubling that Sirhan was waiting in the perfect place with a loaded gun."

We were both quiet, as we calculated the loss our nation had suffered.

Lisa put her hand on mine. "All of the stuff you hear about President Kennedy's murder in Dallas is mind-blowing. Where does it all come from? Do you believe in a big conspiracy?"

"No, I don't. Some deranged person can randomly strike and change history. Lee Harvey Oswald, James Earl Ray, and now Sirhan Sirhan. I think that's too much for most of us to deal with. We have to believe that there's some kind of reason for everything. It's too unsettling to contemplate life being changed forever by the random act of some misfit. How many men will die in Vietnam because Bobby died? The war will continue…"

"Let's talk about something happy," Lisa said brightly. She walked to a coffee pot and styrofoam cups against the wall of the conference room. "Want some coffee?"

"Sure."

"One sugar, no cream, right?"

"You've been paying attention."

She smiled at the comment and poured two cups of coffee. "Mom and Dad will get here tomorrow. It'll be so good to get moved into my apartment and stop living out of a suitcase. Plus, I'm excited for my parents to meet you."

"I'm happy you're gonna get settled in. Your apartment is a real gem," I responded. "I'm looking forward to meeting your parents… but I'm kind of nervous."

Lisa squeezed my hand and then gently rubbed my cheek with the back of her hand. "You? Nervous? I'd say you're the most fearless person I know. I've told them—particularly my mother—all about you."

"How is your dad moving all your stuff up here, since he specializes in two-seater classic sports cars?"

"He also has this big International Harvester Travelall, which is about the size of a small aircraft carrier. It's a classic."

"Of course, it is."

"They're going to arrive Friday afternoon. Can you get away?"

"Just name the time, and I'll be there. Let's go out on the town and take them to someplace cool for dinner."

"That's your department. You figure out a place to go eat. I'm pretty sure you and my dad are going to hit it off big time. He's this bon vivant guy, who loves restaurants, art, history, politics, classic cars, and baseball."

"He sounds like my kind of guy. Are they driving all the way from San Diego to San Francisco in one day. That's a killer."

"No, my sister and her husband live in Santa Barbara. They'll stop there, both coming and going."

"Help me out. You've got two sisters, right?"

"Right. Julia's the youngest and is married. She's the one in Santa Barbara. My other sister, Bridget, lives in San Diego and is working on her master's."

"Hmmm. What do your parents think about our relationship? Do they think it's too quick? Do I need to be nervous?"

"Not at all. They're going to love you."

"I've got to sneak away and get a haircut this afternoon so they don't think I live in Haight Ashbury."

"Why?"

"Because I haven't had a haircut since April when I hit the campaign trail. When Brenda saw me in LA, she told me I looked like Jim Morrison, but I think I'm starting to look like Yvonne DeCarlo."

Lisa started laughing. "You do not. I love your hair. Let me cut it for you tonight. Just a little trim here and there. I don't want you to go to someone like John's 'bird' and come back looking like one of Herman's Hermits.

20

THE PROFESSOR

San Francisco – Friday, June 14, 1968

Lisa called me at the office Friday afternoon to inform me that her parents had arrived at the Hilton and I should come as soon as I could.

When I entered the hotel lobby, I spotted Lisa and her parents, sitting around a table at the bar, having a drink. Lisa's mother, Nancy, was more blonde than her daughter and smaller in stature. She was an attractive, lively looking woman, wearing a blue sleeveless dress with a white sweater tied around her shoulders. Her eyes seemed to twinkle with mischief.

Lisa's father, Gordon, was tall and slender, balding, with thin reddish hair, which had gone mostly gray. He had tortoise shell glasses, was wearing a long-sleeved white shirt and a corduroy jacket—looking every inch a college professor.

They brightened as they saw me walking across the lobby towards the bar. Lisa ran to greet me and put her arm through mine to walk me over to her parent's table.

"Mom and Dad, this is Alex," she introduced.

Gordon shook my hand, and Nancy embraced me.

"It's nice to meet you," I said. "I've heard so much about you."

Nancy gave me an impish look and observed, "You couldn't possibly have heard more about us than we've heard about you."

Lisa gave Nancy a stern glance and said simply, "Mom…"

After exchanging pleasantries, it was revealed that Gordon wanted to drive Lisa's TR-3 to dinner. Nancy bristled and proposed taking the Travelall so we could all ride together, but Gordon reminded her it was packed with Lisa's furniture and boxes in the parking garage.

I intervened. "Why don't we just take two cars. I'll drive my car and take Nancy. Lisa and Gordon can follow in the TR-3." Gordon gave the sly smile of someone who had just won an argument, and he loved my proposal. Nancy seemed to jump at the chance to have some time alone with me.

But Lisa warned me, "I don't know where we're going, so make sure you don't lose me."

"We're going to Ghirardelli Square. There are nice restaurants, and of course, it's the old chocolate factory. It's over a 100 years old and has a great view of San Francisco Bay," I explained. "And of course, there's lots of chocolate shops."

"Ooooh, sounds like heaven to me," Nancy said.

"Just don't lose me," Lisa reiterated.

I put my arm around her and smiled. "Don't worry, sweetheart. You know what kind of car I have. I'll not be traveling at a high rate of speed. We'll just drive down the Embarcadero. At the end of Fisherman's Wharf, you'll see a big brick building, and that's it."

"How will I know which brick building?" Lisa pressed.

"It's the one with like twenty-foot-high neon letters 'G-H-I-R-A-R-D-E-L-L-I,'" I smirked. "I promise I won't lose you."

I led Nancy to my VW Beetle.

"This is so cute," she said.

"I much prefer Lisa's car, but mine is utilitarian. It's good in the crazy San Francisco traffic, even though at times I'm not sure I have enough oomph to get to the top of some of these hills," I said, as I kept an eye on the rear-view mirror, watching for Lisa's car to emerge from the parking garage.

"Cars are practically a religion in our family as you may have guessed."

"There she is," I chuckled as I pulled out in traffic and we were on our way.

Nancy got right down to business.

"I just want you to know you've brought about an amazing change in Lisa. I know it's been just a short time, but much to my husband's chagrin, I talk to Lisa every day. I'm going to have some whopper phone bills. Lisa doesn't talk about anything but you. She's always been a serious-minded, smart girl, but now she's very smitten with you. It's great to see her like this. I hope I'm not overstepping my bounds or wrongly assuming how you feel about her…"

I laughed. "I don't know how to explain it. I've been told by a friend to just let it happen. I know it's only been a couple of weeks. Maybe some people would think I'm crazy, but I don't care. I've fallen in love with Lisa. She's all I think about. As soon as we were together, it's like something just… I don't know… something just clicks," I said as I checked the rearview mirror again.

"Tell me, Nancy. Do you believe in love at first sight?"

She looked thoughtful but before she could answer I said, "I used to say no, but that was before I met Lisa. I was sitting in my hospital room, all alone, and thinking that my life was such a waste…"

"Your life? A waste! How could you think that?"

"I was in a really dark place. Then the door opened; Lisa walked in; and I haven't been the same since. All of those negative thoughts vanished. I'll tell you frankly I feel very exposed, very much at risk, and vulnerable. That makes me sound like a love-struck teenager, but I—"

Nancy chuckled and cut me off. "I don't think you have anything to worry about, Alex."

"I'm glad to hear that." I looked at her and smiled. "During our weekend at the Ambassador Hotel, Lisa was a great comfort to me. I told her things—things from my past I'd never told anyone. It seems so natural with your daughter."

We pulled into Ghirardelli Square and parking karma was with us as we found two open spots together. Lisa and Gordon continued to sit in the car, intently fiddling with something on the dashboard, while Nancy and I exited my car, taking in the view of the Bay and the skyline.

"What a delightful place," Nancy cooed. She put on her sweater. "We San Diego people are wimps. It feels damp and chilly in San Francisco."

I offered her my arm, and we began to walk together towards the building. She looked over her shoulder and waved at Lisa and Gordon to join us. Finally, they caught up to us inside the restaurant. It was a perfect night to walk around the shops and drink in the ambiance of the old building.

As the restaurant hostess led us to our table, Lisa arched her eyebrow and whispered, "Looks like you really turned the charm on my mother. What did you two talk about?"

"Take a wild guess."

We began some lighthearted banter about the history of the square and began talking about Lisa's new apartment. Suddenly there was a loud *pop—pop—pop* sound directly behind me which brought our conversation to an abrupt halt. A busboy had dropped three wine glasses which shattered on the cement floor.

I nearly jumped out of my skin and almost knocked over my ice water.

Lisa put her hand on my shoulder tenderly, "Easy does it, baby."

I nodded and closed my eyes, trying to regain my composure. "I apologize."

"Alex has trouble with sudden popping sounds," Lisa explained. "They bother him a lot right now."

Gordon and Nancy both gave sympathetic looks. "That's very understandable, considering everything that has happened to you," he said, and Nancy nodded.

"You know I tell people I don't remember hearing the shots in the hotel pantry," I confessed. "But I do. It seemed like the shots went on forever."

Gordon continued, "You've had quite an adventure the last few years. What a life!"

I gave a nervous laugh. "Yes, I have. However, I don't mean to be patronizing, but I'm pretty envious of your life. Restoring English sports cars, a professor of History and Political Science, writing books, living in San Diego... I believe you're who I want to be when I grow up."

"I don't think I can match the things you've been through," Gordon responded. "You can speak with some authority about Vietnam and politics. I'm sure you've got some books in you about your experiences."

"How many books have you written?" I asked.

"Two, and formulating a third," Gordon said as the waiter interrupted and took our order for a round of cocktails, while we continued to absent-mindedly peruse the menus.

Lisa began chattering with Nancy about her new apartment. "I'm so glad that I have a small garage down the alley, where I can park my car and get it off the street."

"And I love your view of downtown and the bridge."

After our orders were placed, Nancy removed her reading glasses and commented, "As an English teacher, I'd have to say 1968 plays like a Shakespearean tragedy—so sad. We're still numb about the assassination. Dr. King. The war. It's hard to believe what has happened so far this year. and it's only June. I can only imagine how you feel, Alex."

"Numb is a good word," I said. "After what Lisa and I experienced together at the hospital and at the hotel, we had... well, we experienced some very intense events that we will never forget. We really bonded. Staying in the hotel together was like 20 dates or something."

"That's for sure," Lisa chimed in. "We shared historic events. You know Alex is starting to get strange phone calls from people who say they know 'the truth' about what really happened. People, including my landlord, recognize Alex's name. They say 'hey, weren't you the newspaperman from San Francisco who was wounded in the assassination?' He's something of a celebrity."

"I doubt that," I said shyly.

"Are you kidding me! My first day at work was Alex's triumphant return from Los Angeles. I've never seen anything like it. When Alex walked in the door, they all stopped working, and everyone in the office gave him a standing ovation. It was like… like the Beatles arriving in New York in 1964."

Gordon and Nancy started laughing.

"A standing ovation!"

"That's impressive," Nancy commented.

"Complete with screaming girls, I might add," Lisa joked, as she used her index finger for emphasis. "All of the women in the office were all misty eyed. They kept asking me if I'd met Alex. I played it cool, but I wanted to say, 'Yeah, we shacked up in the Ambassador Hotel last weekend.'"

The O'Dowds laughed, while I rolled my eyes.

Lisa wouldn't let it go. "The women kept saying, 'Oh, Alex!' 'Alex is so wonderful—have you met Alex?' Kiss, kiss, hug, hug. When the gaggle of women cleared away, Alex had their eye makeup and lipstick all over him."

"Now, she's exaggerating…" I said, as I took a sip of my drink.

"I'm detecting an edge in Lisa's voice," Gordon commented. "You sound kind of jealous, dear."

"I think you're right, Gordon," I quipped, "but Lisa has sharp elbows. She's very capable of standing up for herself."

"Okay, if you're all going to gang up on me, I definitely need another drink," Lisa said, raising her empty cocktail glass to signal to a new waiter who went bustling by our table.

"Can I see some photo ID, ma'am?" the waiter asked.

We all smiled, and Lisa proudly produced her California driver's license. "Aren't you the sweetest man ever!" she said to the waiter.

"Wait, wait," I said grabbing her driver's license as the waiter passed it back to Lisa. "I've never seen this picture."

I wrestled it away over her protests. "Geez, look at you. That's not fair. You even look beautiful in a DMV picture."

"Hang onto this one, Lisa," Nancy jested.

I noticed her birthday was October 21, 1941. "Nineteen forty-one—there's an interesting year, Gordon."

"A year that will live in infamy, to be sure," Gordon began.

"Don't get him started," Nancy cautioned.

"But we got Lisa," I retorted. "Something good happened in that year. So, tell me about your books."

Lisa jumped in, about to make a comment on her driver's license, when Gordon jokingly cut her off, "Haven't I taught you to never interrupt anyone who wants to talk about my books?"

"Here we go," Nancy said, with an eye roll, as she and Lisa started a sidebar conversation.

"I wrote one book about William McKinley and another about the overthrowing of Queen Liliuokalani as the monarch of Hawaii by our government and a bunch of American businessmen who wanted to corner the sugar markets. There was actually a coup with Marines landing on Oahu and the whole bit. I stumbled onto that little historical gem while I was researching McKinley. That occurred while McKinley was president."

"Amazing! Why those two topics?" I asked.

"I look for great untold stories or more precisely—*under* told stories. These fit the bill. Most Americans couldn't tell you two sentences about either topic," Gordon proclaimed.

"I fancy myself as something of a history buff, but I'm largely ignorant of these events," I admitted. "Sounds like I need to read your books."

"You'd find the story of Leon Czolgosz very interesting."

"The guy who assassinated McKinley, right? How do you pronounce his name?"

"Basically, ignore the 'C' and say 'zol' then 'gosz.'"

I practiced, and the professor approved.

"Correct. There are real parallels to Sirhan. Czolgosz was an anarchist and considered McKinley to be a symbol of oppression. Czolgosz said he stalked and killed the president for the good of the country. In 1901, the day before the assassination, he wanted to kill McKinley, but he couldn't get close enough to get a good shot.

But despite what had happened to Presidents Lincoln and Garfield, McKinley had little or no security," Gordon recounted.

"Just like Bobby's campaign," I commented. "The campaign didn't want security to get between Senator Kennedy and the crowds—even after what happened in Dallas."

"Exactly what McKinley said. It was McKinley's fondness for pressing the flesh that did him in," Gordon continued, dismissively waving his hand. "Czolgosz's opportunity came the next day as McKinley shook hands with well-wishers at the Temple of Music exhibit in Buffalo. It was a small caliber handgun just like Sirhan used. McKinley hung on for a week before dying from the assault. McKinley actually died of gangrene. I'm sure he would have recovered from his wounds with modern medicine."

"I'll be damned," I exclaimed. "There *are* a lot of parallels. Lisa and I have been talking about the people who insist these type of events are part of a big conspiracy, like JFK in Dallas. I've thought about it a lot. It's seems to be too much for us to accept that a loner misfit can randomly act because he wants to be famous. Oswald wanted to be remembered."

"One interesting footnote was after Czolgosz was executed, they threw sulfuric acid into his coffin in an attempt to erase him."

I shook my head in amazement. "They didn't want him remembered."

"Precisely," Gordon agreed. He pulled an after-dinner cigar out of his pocket and offered me one, but I declined. When he lit it, Lisa gave him a disapproving scowl.

"Lisa's not crazy about my stogies. Right now I've been researching the presidency of Grover Cleveland. As I'm sure you know, he was the only president with two nonconsecutive terms. I find the beginning of the 20th Century to be very interesting. There seems to be a big hole in the public mind between the end of the Civil War and World War I."

Lisa gave her father a sour look as he blew his cigar smoke into the air. Gordon ignored her and continued, "Speaking of World War I, one of the strangest twists of fate involved the assassination of Archduke Franz Ferdinand and his wife in Sarajevo. As you know, it's generally thought to be the spark that started World War I. Someone threw a bomb at the open convertible car, but it missed the royalty. Then a few hours later, the driver of their car got lost and essentially made a u-turn in front of a restaurant where the failed assassin was eating. He rushed outside and shot them both!"

"You know," I began, "a common thread in all of these assassinations is little or no security. One night recently, I was having a beer with a couple of reporters who were covering Bobby's campaign. There had been huge crowds that day, rushing Kennedy's car pulling and tugging on him. These are tough, hardened guys, but we all thought the crowds were frightening. One of my colleagues remarked, 'Those crowds are so out of control. There could be people who want to hurt Bobby, and it gives them an open invitation.' It takes just one crazy person…"

Gordon started to respond, but Lisa intervened. "Okay, you two. You have to talk to us now."

It was a great evening, and Lisa seemed very pleased. Her parents were fascinating. I spent Saturday with them as we hauled Lisa's belongings up the narrow, steep steps to the second and third floors of the townhouse apartment.

The O'Dowds left on Sunday, and I spent the day helping Lisa set up her new digs.

We positioned the couch so that it had a perfect view of the Bay Bridge and San Francisco Bay. We sat there as the city lights began to take over the night. The city lights were beginning to come on.

I opened the bottle of champagne the O'Dowds brought for a house warming gift. Lisa found two champagne glasses and filled them. We clinked our glasses together.

"To many wonderful evenings together, looking at the view of this beautiful city," Lisa toasted.

21

SURPRISING BRENDA

San Francisco - July 1968

It had now been one month since the assassination of Robert F. Kennedy.

Lisa continued to be the only tonic preventing me from being perpetually despondent about the events of the summer. I was still showing Lisa around San Francisco, and we couldn't seem to get enough of one another.

On a beautiful summer evening, I took Lisa to the waterfront for a seafood dinner. As I was walking along Fisherman's Wharf, holding Lisa's hand, I heard a familiar voice calling me. "Alex! Hey, Alex!"

I turned to see Brenda waving her arm wildly as she sat with her husband, Tom, having a drink at an outdoor table in one of the jammed-packed restaurants.

"Brenda! Tom!" I responded as I moved towards them, still holding Lisa's hand, pulling her along. I shook Tom's hand and hugged Brenda while Lisa stood by.

"Can you join us for a drink?" Brenda bubbled. "Have you had dinner? I've been trying to catch up with you."

I looked at Lisa, and she nodded. "We just had dinner, but we'd love to have a drink."

We settled in at their table, and Brenda was wide eyed and smiling. I knew that look.

She extended her hand towards Lisa. "I'm Brenda Romano."

"I'm Lisa O'Dowd. You probably don't remember me, but we met briefly in Los Angeles—at the hospital when Alex dictated his story and I typed it."

"Oh, yes, yes, yes! Of course! I do remember!" Brenda exclaimed. "Duh? I'm embarrassed. I should have recognized you. It took me a minute to remember. Nice to see you again. You're in San Francisco now...?"

I intervened. "Lisa has just moved to San Francisco and is now working at the AP bureau."

Brenda nodded her head. "Aaah, I see."

"It's good to see you again, Alex," Tom said warmly. "You seem to be doing well."

"I am," I replied. "You might say I'm kind of trying to restart my life, and the wounds I got in the assassination are nearly healed— the physical wounds anyway."

A waiter interrupted, and we ordered a round of drinks. Lisa got a cocktail, and I got a single Jack Daniels on the rocks. The waiter turned to Tom and Brenda. "We just got these," Tom said pointing to their drinks.

"But check back, I plan to have some more," Brenda quickly added, as we all laughed.

Brenda wasted little time cutting to the chase. "So are you two..." she said, as she moved her index finger in a circular motion.

"Able to wiggle our fingers?"

"Hilarious, Alex—always with the wisecracks," Brenda responded sarcastically while Tom laughed..

"Lisa and I are not good at being coy, we're seeing one another. We're trying to keep it on the QT in our office, but it seems to be the worst kept secret in San Francisco. You guys know about that. You could say we're a couple."

"I'd say so," Lisa agreed. "In a short time, we've been through quite a bit together that has really solidified our relationship and I'm loving San Francisco."

"That's so great," Brenda gushed, her blue eyes sparkling like freshly poured champagne at the thrill of unearthing a nugget of gossip. "I've tried to call you a few times after I got back from LA, but no one was ever home."

"That's probably because I was with Lisa." I laughed.

"I guess you're right," Brenda responded. "Of course, we've been gone too. Tom and I went to Hawaii to celebrate our anniversary."

"That explains it," I joked. "You two look very tan, and I know you didn't get that way in San Francisco."

"Ah, congratulations," Lisa added. "Alex and I look like vampires compared to you two. Alex has been in the hospital, and I'm a redhead from Southern California."

"Are you from Los Angeles?" Tom asked.

"I grew up in San Diego, then I went to UCLA. I have worked in LA for nearly ten years," Lisa explained. "I always say it's God's cruel joke on me. I grew up with a bunch of girls who look like the ones the Beach Boys sing about—tan California girls with 'bushy, bushy blonde hairdos', and I was the red-haired girl, sitting on the beach, under an umbrella."

Brenda chuckled and then starting telling us about their Hawaii trip.

I noticed Lisa started rubbing her arms as the sun was setting. I could tell she was getting cold in her yellow sundress. I took off my sport coat and put it around her shoulders. That brought an approving smile from Brenda.

"I'm still getting used to San Francisco weather," Lisa explained, pulling my jacket tighter around her.

Brenda then switched gears. "So what happened in LA after I left? When did you get out of the hospital?"

"By the way, before I fill you in on those details…" I said looking at Tom, "I can't thank you enough for flying Brenda down to check on me. It was incredibly kind and generous."

"It was the least I could do. What a horrible tragedy," Tom said quietly. "Brenda and I are still trying to get over Bobby's death."

"So are we. After Brenda went home, Lisa and I went back down to the kitchen pantry. I showed her where it all happened in detail, and we saw the bullet holes. I found the place where I fell and the spot where Sirhan was hiding."

"Oh, my God!" Brenda exclaimed putting her hand to her chest.

"It was very traumatic for Alex," Lisa chimed in.

I then rehearsed an edited timeline of events which transpired after Brenda had left. Tom and Brenda listened intently, often with pained expressions on their faces.

Soon we finished off the drinks and our stories from Los Angeles. "We'd better get going," I announced.

As we were breaking up the party, while Lisa chatted with Tom, Brenda flashed her eyes at me and put her fist to her ear mouthing the words "call me."

Later that night, I dialed Brenda's number.

"Is it too late?"

"Too late! Are you kidding me? I was sitting here getting pissed at you because you hadn't called me yet," she said. "Tell me all about Lisa."

"Lisa stopped by the hospital the day after you left to see how I was doing. The first question she asked was, "Is your wife still here?'"

"No way! What did you say?"

"I tried to explain the mix-up about everyone assuming you were Mrs. Hurley and how we weren't married any more. It just so happens I was being discharged from the hospital the day Lisa dropped by. Since I had not eaten anything except the scrumptious hospital food you and I consumed, Lisa took me to lunch at a burger joint on Wilshire. Then she gave me a ride to the hotel, where I had a room waiting for me..."

"Yeeeess... and... and..."

"Don't get excited, but she did spend the weekend with me at the hotel."

"Pretty groovy little set up, huh?"

"I'd say so. No sex but lots of kissing. Yeah, pretty groovy set up. Phil got me a big suite, and Lisa helped me through all of this ugliness… like going to the scene of the crime and watching the funeral. She was wonderful company. It's strange. It just seems like we belong together. I mean, I'm only happy when I'm with her."

"Wow! That sounds serious. She's very pretty. You look like a different person now. You seemed to have lightened up a bit. You seem so happy."

"In fairness… there wasn't much to be happy about when I saw you last."

"Oh, no doubt about that, but when I saw you walking down the street, holding Lisa's hands, you sure looked content. It made me feel good to see you finding some peace and happiness…" Brenda broke off, and I heard Tom's voice in the background. Then she laughed. "Tom says to tell you that you have good taste in women."

I chuckled and said. "I agree. You know, I never believed in love at first sight. I always thought having a romance with someone in your office is a very bad idea. But…"

Brenda laughed. "I always felt the same way about romances at work. They can end very badly, but when I met Tom, all of that didn't matter anymore. I was willing to risk it, and I just wanted to be with him. Love makes you do crazy things. I believe you can meet a person, and something just happens that you can't explain. It's like this person is a missing piece of you."

"That's exactly how it feels. However, I also feel like a teenager asking the prettiest girl in your school to the prom. I'm afraid she'll say no or that she won't like me as much as I like her. So far so good, though… I can't think about anything else but her."

Brenda sighed. "That's a good sign, but don't over analyze things. You have a tendency to do that, Alex. I believe all of these twists and turns in our lives have happened for a reason."

"Um, hm, I'm starting to believe that too."

"What are the odds that she stops by and that things happened the way they did in LA? Relax, Alex. Don't be afraid to be happy. You deserve it. Just let this thing with Lisa develop. It was so great to see you with her tonight."

LETTER FROM VIETNAM

San Francisco - July 1968

A couple of days later after lunch, I stopped by Lisa's desk.

"When you get a minute, come and see me. I have something to show you."

She put her purse in a desk drawer and followed me. I reached into my sport coat pocket and retrieved a letter from my brother Jay.

Her face flushed when she realized what I had just handed to her.

Dear Alex,

I've written to Mom and Dad, but this is my first letter to you. I've been wanting to drop you a note ever since I got to Vietnam.

When I get a chance, I need to resupply my writing materials. Right now it's hard to keep anything dry. It has been pouring rain without stopping. They say it can rain for 40 days and 40 nights here, just like in the Bible when Noah built the ark. I'm sure you know what I'm talking about.

It's hot and sticky and muddy. I've spent the day filling sandbags and building a bunker where mortar fire came in last night. You were right about the artillery fire in the middle of the night. It's the most frightening experience I've ever had. These VCs are relentless little bastards.

We've been digging in positions, spreading out Claymore mines and coils of razor wire for the attack we know is coming.

I try to be brave, but I'm scared every day. Hiking through the thick jungle is so unnerving. You never know what's around the next corner or hiding in the grass right beside you. The VC seems to blend right into the jungle. I want to do my part to fight the Reds, and I'm now putting all of my training to good use. I just hope I live to tell the tale. Some days I feel sure that I'll not be alive this time tomorrow.

When I'm scared, I can hear Dad's voice ringing in my ears, "Don't be a pussy." You and I have heard that all of our lives.

I've never seen Marines like I see here. All the spit and polish is gone. They looked muddy and dirty and unshaven. I guess that's what I'll look like soon. I'm thinking of growing a mustache. What do you think?

Don't let Mom and Dad read my letters to you. I can tell you how I really feel—no bullshit. You've been here and know what I'm talking about. I write way more upbeat letters, especially to Dad. I know you understand why.

I'm sorry I couldn't connect with you before I left, but you were having problems of your own. I hope you're recovering. I'll do my best to not get shot myself. It would be a helluva deal if both Hurley brothers got shot in the same year.

I'm in a place called Cu Chi. You probably know where that is. I think it's about 20 miles north of

Saigon, but I can't make heads or tails of directions in Vietnam.

The North Vietnamese attack and then go down trap doors into the tunnels.

Our mission is going to be to flush a lot of VC out of these tunnels, somewhere around here. Sounds bad. The real war's going to start for me really soon.

Write when you can, because my brother is the best writer on the planet. I'll try to do the same.

I'll never tell another human being what I'm about to say, but I wish I had listened to you when we talked about Vietnam. Take care of my Chevy for me.

J

Lisa took a tissue out dabbing her eyes and shaking her head. "What's this business about the tunnels?"

"It's a bad place. Very bad. The Viet Cong have miles of tunnels in that area. It was one of the staging areas for the Tet Offensive earlier this year. The tunnels are often rigged with explosive booby traps or punji stick pits. It's a very dangerous place. It makes me sick that my brother is going to be there. Why does he have to be there? Why not some supply depot in South Vietnam?"

Lisa noticed a picture on my desk. It was me, Jay, and San Francisco Giants baseball star, Willie McCovey.

"Is this Jay?" she asked.

"Yeah," I said sadly looking at the picture. "That was a few years ago when the Giants had a press day thing at Candlestick Park. I took Jay with me, and he got to meet all of his heroes."

"Willie McCovey, right?"

I smiled and nodded. "I think Jay was 14 or 15 in that picture."

"His coloring is much darker than yours."

"Yeah, he's the spitting image of my dad. Dark hair, dark eyes. I look more like my mother."

"He's a nice-looking kid," Lisa said wistfully. "The Hurley family raised some cute guys." She continued to study the photo and then sighed, "What's happening in our world, Alex?"

As we sat in silence pondering Jay's letter, John popped by and said, "Good, Lisa's here. I have something to show both of you. There's a bloke coming by to see us."

"About what?" I said with a tinge of irritation.

"I can't say right now. Let's meet in the dark room in a few minutes." And then he disappeared, hustling down the hallway.

It was very out of character for blabbermouth John to be so mysterious.

When Lisa and I arrived in the dark room, we found ourselves alone in the red light. We took a seat on some stools at the light table. I looked at her.

"I know that look," she said flirtatiously. "Hey, baby, let's go the dark room and see what develops. You look pretty sexy in this light."

"It's a good thing you and I aren't photographers—we'd never get anything done," I quipped.

Suddenly John came blustering in the door, with a young guy with bushy black hair and black-rimmed glasses.

"This is my chum, Derek Hill. He's a freelance photographer and was at the Ambassador Hotel when the assassination went down. He's got something to show us."

Derek looked around nervously and said to John, "We're alone, right? I hate to be so paranoid, but can we make it so we won't be interrupted?"

"I told the secretary outside that this is a private meeting, and we were not to be disturbed."

John checked his watch, then reached over and flipped the dead bolt lock on the dark room door. "We just had a deadline, so no one should be pounding on the door for a while," John assured him.

Derek began, "Alex, and I'm sorry... Lisa, right?"

"Right," she replied.

"It's a pleasure to meet you. I've actually seen you before, Alex, but I'm sure you don't remember me."

I arched my eyebrows and shot a glance at Lisa.

Derek reached into his camera bag and pulled out two sheets of contact proofs. He placed them on the light table and handed us two magnifiers.

"I had an assignment to photograph the Kennedy victory party in the ballroom."

"Who's the client?" I asked.

"The California Democratic Party. I travel up and down the state doing freelance work. In fact, I'm here in San Francisco to shoot the car show at the Cow Palace this weekend."

"Sorry to get you off track," I said to Derek. "You mentioned you were in the Ambassador ballroom…"

"Yes. Look at this roll of film," Derek instructed as he pointed to one of the strips. Lisa and I scanned the negatives on the light table. All of the photos are of Senator Kennedy's speech after he won the primary. You can see Ethel Kennedy, Roosevelt Grier—various campaign people behind Bobby."

"Right," I said sadly. "This brings it all back."

"Look at the first two photos on this roll," Derek said.

I was temporarily confused, but then I was amazed at what I saw.

"Take a good look." Derek gestured to Lisa.

It took her just a moment before she gasped, "Oh, my God. It's you, Alex!"

The photo showed me lying on the floor and a frightened looking John Greer, hovering over me, trying to shield me.

"John, have you seen this?" I asked.

"Yeah. I confess it brought tears to my eyes. Who loves you, brother?" he said as slapped his chest.

"I'm overwhelmed," I said solemnly.

"I'd be happy to print a couple of that one for you two before I leave."

"I'd really appreciate that, Derek," I said as I couldn't stop looking at this amazing image. I could see the fear and confusion on my face.

"But there's more to the story. I thought the main event was over—I mean the RFK victory speech. I began following Bobby through the double swinging doors into the pantry. I must have been just a couple of feet behind you, Alex. I had used up my first roll and was fumbling to load a new roll. I planned it that way, since I didn't expect anything of note to happen while we were walking through the kitchen. I actually stopped and moved into a space to the left of the entourage following Senator Kennedy. If you recall, Alex, that would have put me on the opposite side of the kitchen from Sirhan, who was crouched down to the right of Bobby."

Lisa and I were riding on his every word, while John made two prints of me on the floor of the pantry.

Derek continued,"By moving towards the steam tables, I had a clear view of Senator Kennedy shaking hands with one of the bus boys. That was probably the last thing he ever did because the shooting started right after that. I had just finished loading a fresh roll when I heard Sirhan yelling, 'Kennedy, you son of a bitch!' I began snapping away as quickly as I could. I had pictures of the shooting, good shots of the bodyguards wrestling with Sirhan, and good pictures of the victims—like you."

Lisa and I were confused.

"But I see only two rolls. Where's the other roll?" she asked.

"Ah, there's the rub. I reloaded another roll and took photos of Alex on the floor. This is actually my third roll in the sequence."

Derek and John exchanged glances. "This roll has the pictures of Alex, a couple of other shooting victims, a woman with a bandaged head and as you can see a bunch of random shots in the ballroom— all the chaos among supporters, as word of the shooting spread."

Lisa grabbed a magnifier and quickly scanned the third roll and handed it to me. It was a bunch of photos of people crying and embracing in the aftermath of the shooting.

"When I was in the ballroom, after the shooting," Derek continued. "I noticed two men in suits watching me. It seemed like if I took two steps away from them, they took two steps towards me. It was obvious they were watching me."

"After Sirhan's attack, right?" I asked.

"Oh, yeah, after. I didn't notice them until after the shooting when I returned to the ballroom. I figured I had documented the speech and the shooting, and I went back to get some reaction shots in the ballroom. When it became clear that they were honed in on me, I panicked and started to run. My only thought at that point was I just wanted to get the hell out of there. When I got outside the hotel, the two guys jumped me and threw me on the ground. They bent one of my arms behind my back and searched my pockets. I thought they were cops and that they were going to arrest me. They took all three rolls of film and my camera."

"I kept yelling, 'I haven't done anything wrong!'" Derek explained.

"How did you get these back?" Lisa asked.

"I assumed they were LAPD detectives. When I offered resistance, one of them punched me in the stomach, knocking me to the ground. As they left, one of them said, 'You can pick your stuff up downtown.'"

"Bastards! Good ole' LAPD," Lisa commented. "I've had a few scrapes with them. My experience has been that they will do whatever they can get away with. They're bullies."

"I went down to the cop shop the next day, and they said they didn't have anything for me, because detectives were still gathering materials from the Ambassador Hotel. I went back the second day, and they gave me two rolls of contact prints, the original film, and my camera. When I protested that I had three rolls of film, I was told the records show I had two rolls and a camera. The clerk said I would need to fill out a form if I wanted to claim any 'lost items.'"

"And the missing roll contains photos taken after shooting started—right?" I surmised.

"You got it. It's impossible to believe this is an accident," Derek said. "I could have a shot on the missing roll that's at least as good as the one from the *LA Times* that you see everywhere—the one of Bobby lying on the floor with the bus boy supporting his head. I may have a photo of the actual shooting."

We sat in stunned silence for a moment.

"What does this mean?" I asked.

"I wish I knew," Derek lamented.

"Have you filled out the claim form for the LAPD?" Lisa asked. "I know it's bureaucratic nonsense, but I think you should. Keep pushing it. If there's some funny business going on—and I think there is— they want to give you the run-around so you'll let it drop. I've got some contacts there. Let me see what I can find out."

"Lisa worked for the UPI in Los Angeles for several years," I explained.

"That'd be great, John's got my phone number if you want to talk. Let me know if you find out something. Thanks for your time," Derek said. "I told John my story over dinner last night, and he said I should talk to you two."

"Thanks, man," I said. "We appreciate you coming by. Take care of yourself."

John and Derek departed, leaving Lisa and I sitting on the stools in the dark room.

"That's a helluva story. Was there something unusual on the second roll, or is it just the LAPD over-reacting?" I asked.

"I dunno. Both things are possible."

On Sunday night, as Derek left the auto show at the Cow Palace, he was hit by a fast-moving car in the parking lot. The police report said two witnesses saw Derek being thrown up over the hood, but they didn't get a look at the car. Derek died instantly. The driver of a dark-colored Ford sedan left the scene and was never found.

23

CONSPIRACIES IN THE SHADOWS

San Francisco, July 1968

Lisa entered the conference room Monday afternoon with a manila folder full of papers and sat down next to me. "How's John doing?"

I shook my head. "I haven't seen him since Sunday night when he stopped by my place to tell me about Derek. He was really unstrung. I've never seen him like that."

Lisa looked at her watch. "I've got an appointment at three that I can't miss. I've been chasing this guy for a week. John's coming in here to talk to us, right?"

"Yeah. He should be here any minute. Who's your three o'clock?"

"It's that city supervisor I told you about who keeps giving me the slip. I think I finally have him cornered."

"Did you get any information from LAPD?"

"I got some information, but I don't know how satisfying it will be," Lisa responded, patting the bulging folder. "You know one of the most frightening things that ever happened to me was at the hands of an LA cop during a traffic stop."

"Frightening?"

"Yeah. Scary. Very scary. I was coming back from San Diego on a Sunday night after spending the weekend visiting my parents and sister. I had just turned off the freeway onto a dark street heading for my house, when out of nowhere these red lights go on behind me. I didn't know what I had done, but I pulled over."

"Uh-oh…"

"I had the top down on the Triumph, and this cop comes to the driver's side door, shines his flash light right in my eyes, and tells me to get out of the car."

I shook my head. I felt like I knew where this story was going, but I hoped I was wrong.

Lisa continued her narrative. "It was a warm summer day, and I was just wearing shorts and a tank top. I stood by my car, and this creep slowly moves his flashlight beam up and down my body checking me out. I knew this wasn't normal and that I was in big trouble. I asked him why he stopped me. He didn't reply. 'I need your license and registration,' he said."

"Did he have a partner with him?"

"Yeah. The creepy cop was older, kind of middle aged, and his partner was this younger guy, who was lingering around the back of my car with a smirky grin on his face. My purse was on the front seat, and I was afraid to turn my back on him."

I caught a glimpse of John hurriedly entering the newsroom, heading for the conference room, but I wanted to hear the rest of Lisa's story. "You still didn't know why he stopped you?" I asked.

"No. I told him I was getting my license out of my purse. I was starting to shake when I turned and reached into my car. I quickly grabbed my license and my UPI press pass."

Now Lisa also saw John heading for the conference room and quickened the telling of her tale. "To make a long story short, the pervert cop shines his flashlight on my license and looks me over again. 'Well, Lisa, you and I could work something out here, so I don't have to give you a ticket.' He looked up and down the street to make sure no one was around. It was dark and quiet. The young cop in the back of the car came forward and stood by me. I thought I was about to get raped or molested."

"How did you get out of that?"

"I flashed my press pass at the cop and said 'How would you like to see the story of this traffic stop on the front page of the *LA Times*? He flinched pretty hard, looked at his partner, and nodded. Then he simply handed me my license, tipped his hat, and said, 'You're free to go, ma'am. Have a nice evening.'"

My mouth was hanging open. "That was a gutsy move on your part."

"It was the only move I had. I was only a couple of years out of college and was young and naive. If a cop did that to me now, I'd have his head on a pike. I got back in my car and waited until they drove away. I started crying and couldn't stop shaking."

"Wow."

John entered the room as I said, "So are we to assume these rogue cops were just out cruising around, hunting for young, pretty girls like you to prey on."

"Apparently. I know wonderful, brave cops. I'd hate to have their job on the streets of Los Angeles, but there are some bad apples. They bully people... I can't imagine how frightening it would be to be a young black man, who mysteriously gets pulled over by the LAPD," Lisa concluded.

I stood and hugged John, who stood by listening to the rest of our conversation. "I'm really sorry about, Derek. How're you doin', man?"

"Didn't sleep at all last night after I talked to you. I got Derek's stuff from the SFPD and tried to find a contact... ya know, like someone in his family or something."

Lisa also embraced John. "It's terrible news. I wish there was something I could say."

"It's just too weird to have this happen, especially after what Derek showed us on Friday afternoon," John said, while he kept his arm around Lisa. "Did you find out anything from down south? I heard you talking about the LAPD when I came in."

"Yeah, let's sit down," Lisa said, as she opened a folder of notes. "I talked to a couple of my reliable sources in the cop shop. These two people would only talk off the record as soon as I mentioned the assassination. There's a task force in the LAPD called SUS."

"SUS?" I asked.

"It stands for Special Unit Senator. It's a group of LAPD investigators, and their job is to keep a lid on the murder case. The brass wants to make sure there's not a lot of conspiracy theories coming out of the assassination," Lisa explained. "Some witnesses, including some well-heeled supporters of Senator Kennedy, have questioned the tactics of the group. They feel the cops called them in and then brow beat them into supporting the conventional version of the assassination."

I was puzzled. "I keep hearing reference to the 'official version' of the assassination. The FBI agents strongly hinted there's more to the story than just Sirhan Sirhan. The feds said I may think I know what's going on but I don't. What is it? What are they talking about?"

"And what does all this have to do with Derek?" John asked impatiently.

Lisa put her hands in the air. "Hang on guys, I'll get to that. There are witnesses who say they saw a second gunman. There are people who claimed that more than eight shots were fired, and we've been hearing the story of the woman in the polka-dot dress…"

"Woman in the polka-dot dress?" John asked.

"There are reports that Sirhan was seen the day of the shooting and later in the pantry in the company of a girl wearing a polka-dotted dress, and they were with another male companion." Lisa flipped open her reporter's notebook. "The woman was described as having dirty blond hair, *'well-built'*—by the way, I love how cops use that phase—translation 'big tits'—with a crooked or 'funny' nose, wearing a white dress with blue or black polka-dots.

"A RFK campaign worker was taking a break out on the balcony, having a smoke, and claims she saw the woman and man run from the hotel shouting, 'We shot him. We shot him.' When the campaign worker asked who they meant, the woman in the polka-dotted dress replied, 'Senator Kennedy.'"

"Bloody hell," John exclaimed. "So the game's up?"

"Even if the story about the woman and her male companion is true, that doesn't mean Sirhan wasn't the lone gunman," I inserted.

"I agree," Lisa agreed. "There were reports of people seeing Sirhan at a shooting range, practicing, prior to the assassination. But here's where it gets good and may explain what happened to Derek's second roll of film. The SUS is interviewing people and leaning on them. My source says some witnesses—including one of the people who claimed to have seen the woman in the polka-dotted dress—have recanted their story."

"How can they get away with that?" John raged, running his fingers through his hair.

"I know I sound like a broken record, but it's because they can," I said. "Lisa was telling me a story like that when you came in."

Lisa nodded agreement. "One of my sources said the SUS task force is gathering up every scrap of evidence so they can control the flow of information and choke off any questions or doubts about what happened in the pantry."

"So you're saying Derek's roll of film ended up in the SUS files?" John queried.

"That would be my guess," Lisa answered softly.

"There's something that bothers me about the whole thing," John lamented. "Bobby Kennedy was shot in the back of the head at point blank range, but Sirhan was in front of him. He came rushing at Senator Kennedy yelling. How did Bobby get shot from behind?"

"I've thought about that a thousand times," I said. "I've come up with two scenarios. It's possible Bobby turned his back to Sirhan in a defensive maneuver to try to get away from him. One of Sirhan's shots hit Bobby in the neck and another in the armpit area. Another possibility is Bobby had turned his back to Sirhan's location so he could reach across a steam table to shake hands with a kitchen worker. All shots entering Senator Kennedy were from behind."

We were all quiet for what seemed like a long time as we turned the events of that horrible night over in our mind.

"Now the big question," John said. "Was Derek murdered because of the things he told us on Friday?"

Lisa looked at me before answering. "I don't know if Alex agrees with me, but here's my two cents: The LAPD already had what they wanted from Derek. I'm very suspicious of coincidences, and I don't trust the cops—particularly the LAPD. However, even the most paranoid version of myself has trouble believing that some shadowy characters followed Derek to San Francisco and killed him because of our discussion on Friday—which was about as private as you can get, hiding out in the dark room."

I looked at the pain on John's face and said, "I have to agree with Lisa. Maybe it's just bad luck… maybe Derek was careless… maybe, maybe, maybe… I just think Derek was in the wrong place at the wrong time Sunday night."

"Bollocks! I want to blame someone for killing Derek, but I guess I have to agree with both of you."

Lisa put her arm around John's shoulder to comfort him as big tears ran down his face. His emotions deteriorated further as he began to shake and sob. "I'm so sorry, John. All of this stuff doesn't change how tragic and sad it was to lose Derek like this."

"Thanks for trying, luv," John said quietly.

We were mum for several minutes while John sniffed and wiped his eyes, trying to regain his composure.

I broke the silence with an announcement. "I got a phone call this morning. I've been subpoenaed to testify at the trial of Sirhan Sirhan."

"What are you going to say?" Lisa asked.

"I have no idea. As John knows, I really didn't see anything. I heard the shots but was it Sirhan firing the gun? Beats me," I said. "It could have been John Wilkes Booth for all I know."

The mysterious circumstances of Derek's death seems to fade as the summer wore on. It was one more alarming event in a seemingly unending bleak procession that defined life in 1968.

Things took an abrupt change in my career and subsequently impacted my relationship with Lisa. I had become accustomed to seeing her several times a day at work and then spending the evening together.

I was offered a job at the *San Francisco Chronicle* as a political columnist and the Assistant Managing Editor of Politics. The surprise offer from the *Chronicle* came like a bolt out of the blue when I met with a couple of the big cheeses from the paper over lunch one day. It was an extraordinary opportunity, which undoubtedly came my way because of the notoriety I gained from my involvement in the assassination.

Lisa and Phil both encouraged me to take the new job. It was truly an offer that couldn't be refused, even though I'd miss my friends and colleagues at the AP Bureau.

At my going-away party, John surprised me with an incredible gift. It was an 8x10 photo of me and Bobby Kennedy. It wasn't a posed picture, but we were standing together talking. Bobby was leaning against a desk with his arms folded looking at me. I believe I was actually interviewing him after his debate with Eugene McCarthy in San Francisco.

John found the photo when he was organizing all of his film from our coverage of the campaign. He put it in a frame for me, and I would put it on my desk at my new job. It instantly became one of my most cherished possessions.

August had been a month of big changes for me and Lisa. We were both settling into our new life and new jobs. Career transitions always seem to turn out to be harder and more stressful than you imagine when you launch your journey.

Lisa was a very capable professional journalist, but she was adjusting to a new city and new work environment. I was getting used to the new culture in the big city daily newspaper and trying to fit in my new role as a columnist and as Assistant Managing Editor of Politics. Frankly, I was still trying to figure out what that new title meant.

Lisa surprised me one evening with some prints of photos John had taken. She said she was on an assignment with John, and they saw an ad with my face on the side of a city bus. The tag line was, "Read Alex Hurley in the *Chronicle*."

Lisa was laughing hysterically as she described John sprinting down the street, loaded with camera equipment, trying to get a picture of the bus with my ad on it. She said John was like a dog chasing a car. Later they discovered a cable car near Fisherman's Wharf that had my photo on the side. John took a picture of Lisa mugging for the camera and blowing a kiss at my photo.

She was spending a lot of time in the Haight Ashbury covering the aftermath of San Francisco's "Summer of Love" last year, when hippies and counter culture people inundated the city. Lisa was writing a series of stories about how Haight Ashbury was coping with the residual impact of hundreds of people with serious drug problems and other social maladies, who now lived permanently in the neighborhood.

Still bubbling under the surface of my psyche was trauma of the assassination and its aftermath. Lisa and I were glued to the TV in the evenings in August, watching the political parties go through the ritual of their conventions.

In a year of horrific events, the Democratic Convention in Chicago was one of the worst moments. Americans sat in their living rooms as summer waned and watched Chicago Police savagely beat antiwar protesters with clubs. It felt like our country was coming apart.

Vice President Hubert Humphrey emerged as the Democratic nominee. Lisa and I speculated for hours about how different the world would be if Robert Kennedy was still alive. This provided plenty of fodder to jumpstart my new career as a political columnist.

Never far from my mind was my brother Jay. Every morsel of news from Vietnam made me wonder what Jay was doing that day. I came to the realization that when you have a loved one in harm's way in the combat zone, their well-being is the first thing you think of in the morning and the last thing you think of as you go to sleep. It made me reflect on what I callously put Brenda through when I left for Vietnam.

The letters provided little comfort. I knew of several people who got letters from their sons or husband or brother after they were already KIA. I got a couple of letters at the end of the summer, and Jay's normally sunny, optimistic persona seemed to fade with each passing week. When I talked with my mother, she would read me the latest letter she had received from Jay, and they were much rosier than the ones I got. I knew my letters were Jay's unvarnished recounting of his time in Vietnam.

Throughout August, I had to get used to the idea of not working side-by-side with Lisa every day, and many days I could only get a few hours with her in the evening. She told me one night over dinner that she had been asked out twice by two different guys who were my former colleagues at the AP Bureau.

I pressed her for their names, and she reluctantly revealed their identity. I admit it—I was instantly jealous, but I couldn't blame them for asking her out. We had tried to keep our relationship a secret, and if I were those guys, I'd ask Lisa out too.

I was comforted that her response was that she had a serious boyfriend and couldn't go out with them.

As the fall began, the ground seemed to continue to move under our feet in seismic shifts that altered the course of our lives.

Then on a rainy Friday night in September everything changed again. It would be a weekend we would never forget.

24

BULLITT

San Francisco - September 1968

W e had excitedly anticipated our Friday night date to attend a sneak preview for the movie that all of San Francisco was waiting to see—*Bullitt,* starring Steve McQueen.

The movie was scheduled to hit the theaters in October, but I pulled a few strings at the *Chronicle* and at the AP Bureau to get two "press" tickets for the studio's premiere for "critics." Lisa was accustomed to such arrangements after being a reporter in Hollywood, and I had been counting the hours until the sneak preview.

After the stories from her landlord, we were anxious to see how much of Lisa's neighborhood made it into the film.

The autumn rains settled in over the city with a vengeance that Friday night, and I ran from my parked car to the steps of Lisa's apartment, trying to take shelter under my umbrella, which was being turned inside out by the gusty winds.

As soon as I entered Lisa's apartment, she greeted me with her usual kiss and helped me deal with my drenched rain coat and umbrella. However, I detected something was different.

"I need to change clothes."

"I missed you today," I said, trying to jump start our evening.

"I missed you too," Lisa replied flatly, with seemingly little enthusiasm. "It's been a long week. Where and when is our movie again?"

"The theater is on Geary Street, and the movie starts at 7." I checked my watch. "It would probably be good to go a little early since parking is always a wild card in that neighborhood."

She nodded and headed upstairs.

"Is there something wrong?"

"No. I wanted to get home earlier to get ready, but that didn't work out. Get a drink if you want," she replied vacantly over her shoulder, as she moved away. Her usual sparkle was missing.

Lisa seemed pre-occupied, like she had something on her mind. Maybe she was tired, but her serious demeanor surprised me. It cast a cloud over my earlier enthusiasm for the premiere.

I stared out the window at the Bay Bridge and the long line of cars lining up like ants at a picnic waiting to crawl onto the bridge for the Friday night commute.

I made myself a drink and noticed it seemed to be taking a while upstairs. I nervously glanced at my watch. I wondered if this Southern California girl knew that the time she spent fussing with her hair would be negated in a few seconds when we stepped outside in the blustery San Francisco wind.

At last I heard her heading down the stairs. She wore black tights, the shortest skirt I'd ever seen her wear and a bright green sweater. Her red hair was pulled back in a ponytail, and she seemed to be wearing more makeup tonight including some pink lipstick.

"Wow, that was worth the wait," I exclaimed.

"Wait? I didn't take too long, did I?"

"No, no. It was just a figure of speech," I said. "You look beautiful."

Her only response was a quick smile before we grabbed our coats and umbrella and headed for the car. I opened the curb side door and let her in. As she slid into the passenger seat, the short skirt enticingly revealed her long shapely legs.

The movie was sensational. We oohed and awed throughout the movie as we recognized locations around the city. Steve McQueen's fictional character—Lt. Frank Bullitt— lived in the dark blue building across the street from Lisa's building and visited the market on the corner to buy some groceries, mostly TV dinners.

There were several interiors shots of Steve McQueen inside the apartment and glimpses of the magnificent Jacqueline Bisset, who played Bullitt's girlfriend, walking around wearing only a pajama top, eating a bowl of cereal for breakfast, while sitting in the bay window.

Lisa and I held hands for much of the movie, and I also gently rubbed my hand over her tantalizingly exposed thighs several times.

Our euphoria over the movie seemed to brighten Lisa's mood, and we chattered excitedly as we drove back to her apartment.

When I pulled up to Lisa's apartment building in the pouring rain, there were no parking spots nearby.

"Steve McQueen parked right there," Lisa joked.

"Unfortunately, I'm not Steve McQueen, and to top it off, there's no parking spot. And my car is definitely not a souped up Mustang. Why don't I let you out? I may have to park around the block, and then I'll come back for a nightcap."

"Okay. You're so sweet." She gave me a quick kiss, jumped out of the car and ran for it.

I found a parking spot around the corner and then made my way back to her apartment. I was surprised that when I tried the door it was locked. I fished my keys out of my pocket and used the spare to open Lisa's door.

When I entered the apartment, the only source of light was a lamp on the end table by the couch. It was quiet, and there was no Lisa.

"Lisa," I called. "Where are you, baby?" I walked into the kitchen and checked the downstairs bathroom, which was dark and vacant. As I re-entered the living room, I took off my wet trench coat and tossed it on the chair. Then I saw Lisa slowly descending the stairs wearing a short, white silky robe. Her hair was loose, resting on her shoulders.

I stood transfixed. In the dim light and her robe and pale white skin made her appear translucent. She began unbuttoning my shirt and when I embraced her I found she was nude under the robe.

"Would you like to come upstairs with me?" she asked softly, as she kissed me.

I aggressively grabbed her and began kissing her neck, while massaging her hips through the thin robe. She gently pushed me away and said, "Take it slow. Come with me."

The rain was pounding with greater ferocity against the windows, as I took her hand and she led me up the narrow staircase. Lisa had turned back the covers on the bed, and the only light came from candles on the two nightstands.

I sat on the edge of the bed and kicked off my shoes and socks, while she closed the bedroom blinds. She stood in front of me in the candlelight, untying her robe, letting it slide off of her shoulders and fall to the floor.

"Do you want me?"

"I've wanted you from the first time I saw you." I looked into her vivid green eyes that seemed moistened by tears. "I love you so, Lisa. I'm so afraid to lose you."

"I love you too. There's never been anyone like you in my life."

I buried my face in her bare breasts, kissing and caressing her.

She immediately responded breathing deeply and sighing, then she stopped me. "Alex, there's something I need to tell you."

That got my full attention.

"It's my first time," she said meekly.

"You are a… you mean this is your first time… having sex? You didn't do it in college or with your boyfriend or…"

"Never. Nobody. Is that all right?"

"Of course…" I murmured as I kissed her earlobe.

I gently pulled her on top of me, and we tumbled onto the bed, making love for the first time. It was well after midnight when we fell asleep in each other's arms.

I have never felt so happy.

25

ROMANCE ON A RAINY MORNING

San Francisco Saturday, September 7, 1968

I don't know what time it was on Saturday morning when I first opened my eyes. I didn't care. I didn't glance at a clock as I usually did, because I was too busy looking at Lisa.

It was quiet. The rain had stopped outside, and Lisa was sound asleep, lying on her back, with her arms extended above her head and her red hair covering part of her face. The sheet covered her from the waist down, but she was on full display to me in the soft morning light.

She took my breath away. It was her first time—a confession that surprised me—but it had been a long time since I had made love to a beautiful woman—and Lisa was the most beautiful woman.

I gently pushed her hair off of her face and rubbed her cheek. I tried not to wake her, but her eyes fluttered, then opened. She smiled sleepily at me as I propped myself up on my elbow next to her.

"Good morning. Give me a second," she whispered.

She got out of bed, and I watched her walk into the bathroom.

As she walked back to the bed, I said, "How are you this morning?"

"I don't think I've ever been better. I'm cold. Can you help get me warm again?" She put her arms around my neck and kissed me.

We burrowed into the covers, and she pushed her body against mine closer and closer, one passionate kiss after another.

I came up for air for a second and said, "I have a question. Believe me, I appreciate your enthusiasm, but since this is where babies come from..."

She interrupted, "I've been on birth control pills for a couple of years to help regulate my periods. We're fine."

Lisa rolled onto her back and pulled me on top of her. We made love again and collapsed in a somewhat sweaty heap on the bed.

Lisa put her head on my chest, and we quietly savored the wonderful moment we were having, wrapped in one another's arms, not talking, not wanting to break the mood... I loved that about her. We could be silent and still feel close to one another. Lisa began lightly rubbing my chest with the tips of her fingers and then gently touched the site of the wound I received in Los Angeles.

"Does it hurt?"

"No. It's tender but seems to be healing. It's been three months since the shooting..." I then wistfully added, "It seems longer, doesn't it?"

"It also seems unreal—like a weird nightmare."

"I assume I'll always have a scar there. It will just be the latest addition to a collection of wounds on my body. I'm like a high-mileage vehicle. I was once shiny and new, but now there's a lot of wear and tear."

Lisa giggled and gave me a kiss. "Oh, Alex."

"I'm sorry. I wish I had a beautiful, flawless body like you."

"Hardly," Lisa said.

"Your skin is like porcelain. You're perfection. Your hips, your breasts, your legs... you are so pretty."

She kissed me. "What are those two scars on your back?"

"Souvenirs from Vietnam. I was walking on a ridge line, and a mortar shell landed nearby. The concussion from the blast sent me flying in air, falling head over heels down a ravine. The only way I stopped was by crashing into a tree. That was another time I thought I was going to die. I spent a couple of weeks in a hospital.

It was then that the AP and the Army decided I'd had enough fun and sent me home."

"My poor baby. I want you to stay healthy. Don't ever leave me, Alex. I can't imagine not having you now. I've been worried I wouldn't handle our relationship right—that I'd screw things up. That's why I was so uptight last night. I planned to take a big step and make love for the first time, and I was worried."

"Worried?"

"The plan I had—I guess I was trying to entice you and make it romantic. I'm not very good at seduction scenes like that."

"You could have fooled me. I was wondering what was going on last night. I became concerned. You seemed so pre-occupied."

"You're right. I had a lot on my mind when you got here last night. I got home later than I thought, so it threw me off." Lisa reached for her robe on the floor by the bed. "Do you want some coffee or anything?"

"Let's make a new rule that we have to spend the weekend in this apartment… and you can't wear clothes."

Lisa laughed. "Making hot coffee when naked makes me nervous."

I ignored her joke and made a confession. "You know I've been so insecure about our relationship. Despite all of your reassurances and things your mother said, I've been afraid that I'm going to make a wrong move and that you're going to dump me."

"Dump you? Just the opposite is true. I've become very dependent on you, and I want to be part of all of your free time. I haven't liked it since you left the AP, and I can't see you as much."

"I just want you, Lisa. I never believed in love at first sight and all that nonsense, until I met you."

Lisa kissed me again. "I've thought about nothing else for days and how badly I want to give myself to you."

She sat on my lap, and I held her for a few moments. Lisa finally broke the silence as she stood and ran her fingers through her long red hair. "Go take your shower, and I'll be back with some coffee."

I wrapped a towel around my waist after my shower and sat in the chair next to the bed as Lisa ascended the stairs with two cups of coffee.

"Things will never be the same after last night," I began.

"I know. That's what I've been thinking about all week," she said, as she sat on the edge of the bed and carefully took the first sip of her hot coffee.

"By the way, I love that robe. It shows off your beautiful, long legs. And that skirt you wore last night—it really blew me away."

"I tried. I've always had an issue with my legs… or more specifically being tall."

"I don't think of you as being so tall. I'm 5-11, and what are you 5-8 or 5-9?"

Lisa rolled her eyes. "5-10. I don't think I've grown an inch since 7th or 8th grade. I was always the big, gawky girl in the back row of class pictures. The boys seemed attracted to the cute, little girls. I was what is politely called a 'late bloomer.'"

"You? I don't believe it."

"I'll show you some old pictures sometime, and then trust me—you'll believe it!"

I put down my coffee on the nightstand and knelt on the floor in front of Lisa. She put her coffee on the tray in anticipation of some rowdy behavior.

"Lisa, I can't imagine sleeping alone now. I want to see you when I open my eyes in the morning, and I want to hold you every night as I go to sleep."

She ran her fingers through my hair and looked tenderly at me. "What are you suggesting?"

"Will you marry me?"

She gasped, but I continued, rapidly getting my proposal out as if she might stop me at any moment..

"I'd like to marry you right away, but if you're not quite ready, I can wait. I want you. You are the only woman I'll ever want. I can wait, if I have to, and…"

She interrupted with a smile. "Alex, shush. Do I get to answer?"

"Sorry."

"Of course, I'll marry you."

As I knelt in front of her, she spread her legs, and I buried my head in her chest. She tenderly caressed me.

"Everything has happened so fast," she said softly. "I've always thought I was very deliberate about major decisions, but with you, there seems to never be any doubt in my mind."

"I've been a mess since I met you. I can't concentrate on anything. I'll admit, I was nervous when you arrived here in the city. I was worried that the wonderful feelings we had in LA wouldn't transfer to San Francisco."

"You just gave a perfect description of my feelings…" She kissed me lightly above my eyebrow. "I'm gonna jump in the shower, and then I'll make some breakfast."

I smiled and nodded as I stacked the pillows on the bed and then reclined. "Can I watch?"

She gave me a coquettish smile and dropped her robe on the bed before heading to the shower. She looked in the mirror and tied her hair up with a red ribbon. Her shower had an opaque shower curtain, and I watched her gingerly test the water before climbing in.

When she stepped out of the shower, she looked sheepishly at me. "I've never had a man watch me take a shower."

"I'm very glad to hear that."

"You make me feel self-conscious," Lisa said, blushing, as she wrapped herself in a towel as she got out of the shower. She walked towards me, dropped the towel, and put her white robe back on.

"If only you could see yourself through my eyes…"

I got off the bed and stood behind her. I started kissing her neck and reaching inside her robe to gently rub her. She responded, but breathlessly said, "If you keep touching me like that, we'll never get breakfast made."

"I don't care."

"We need to come up for air at some point." She took my hand and led me downstairs. "Let's call my parents after breakfast and give them the news."

I smiled and nodded.

Lisa seemed so comfortable around me with no hint of self consciousness. I sat in a nearby chair watching the sexy object of my desire sprawled on her bed like a Playboy model exposing herself to me while she excitedly chatted with her parents. It was overwhelming.

Lisa glanced at her alarm clock before placing the call. It was almost 11 a.m.

Lisa's phone was on the nightstand by her bed. She excitedly dialed her parents. "Hi, Mom. Get Dad on the extension."

"What have I been doing this morning?" she repeated, with a sly smile on her face.

I teasingly put my index finger to my lips, suggesting the goings on in her apartment are a secret.

She returned a smile at my gesture and winked. "Alex is here… oh, hi, Daddy… We have some exciting news. Alex and I are getting married!"

I could hear whoops and hollers from San Diego in reaction to the news.

Lisa excitedly talked about our evening together and about how much of her neighborhood made it into the movie *"Bullitt."* She told them we had a "romantic night together." Then, she cut to the chase and said, "We talked about how we always wanted to be together and then Alex popped the question, and it all just seems so normal—just like everything has been between the two of us."

Lisa filled in more details, but left the passionate love-making part to her parents' imagination. As she explained our decision to merge our lives, the magnitude of what had happened in the last 12 or so hours began to sink in with me.

I was the luckiest man in the world for those moments. In the back of my mind, I envied the conversation she was having with her parents and contemplated how my mom and dad would react in a few minutes.

Lisa handed me the phone and said her parents wanted to talk to me. They gushed their congratulations and welcomed me to the family. I told them how lucky I was, not only to have Lisa, but also how fortunate I was to be in their family.

After we hung up, Lisa said they were okay with the quick city hall marriage idea, and they planned to throw a big shindig in San Diego with all of their friends and Lisa's friends from LA. It all sounded great.

"We have lots of plans to make," Lisa said, "but we should call your parents."

"Yeah, let's do." I picked up the phone and dialed their number. It rang for a while, and I was about ready to hang up but then my dad answered. There was a subliminal flash in my brain that something was wrong. My father never answered the phone.

I said, "Hi, Dad. It's Alex."

"Where the hell have you been? I've been trying to get you all morning."

There was an uncomfortable silence. "Dad, what's wrong?"

"It's Jay. A chaplain and a Marine came to the door this morning."

"Oh, no. Please, no…" I cried, gasping for air, and Lisa rushed towards me with a look of alarm.

"Jay was killed in Vietnam," my dad announced solemnly.

26

LET IT BE

The rest of that weekend was a blur.

Following the pattern for 1968, any moments of joy were quickly countered by some unthinkable, soul-crushing tragedy.

I had never felt happier than I did that morning in Lisa's bedroom. Then, the news of my brother's death weighted my heart with a sorrow so heavy I couldn't breathe. Later that day, we drove to my parents' house in Walnut Creek and tried to comfort one another. Lisa and I also broke the news about our pending marriage.

My parents were very gracious to her, especially considering the circumstances. My mother sat on the couch, clutching a 8x10 framed photo of Jay in his Marine uniform. Lisa sat by my mother, who began telling her story after story about Jay as a kid.

Meanwhile, I walked into the kitchen and sat down at the table with my dad. He pulled a can of Schlitz out of the refrigerator and then gestured with a grunt, offering me a beer. I nodded. It occurred to me how many times throughout my life I wanted to sit at the kitchen table with my dad, share a beer, and talk about life. Finally, the moment had arrived.

I didn't want to say the wrong thing and treaded carefully. "Any details about Jay?"

My dad took a long chug of the beer and sighed deeply. His eyes were rimmed with redness. I had never seen him like this.

"The damn gooks ambushed his unit while they were clearing these tunnels, where the VC retreated after their attacks. I'm sure it was very quick. Jay probably never knew what hit him."

I had seen terrible suffering of wounded men before they died in Vietnam. These wounded soldiers most definitely knew what hit them, but I said simply, "You're probably right. I saw it firsthand when I was over there. The VC are really good at these hit-and-run attacks."

My dad nodded.

"That's a pretty lady you have there," my dad commented. "Do you think she'll make you happy?"

"I do."

Then something happened that never had before. My dad offered me some solace—some empathy.

"You've been through a helluva lot this summer. I hope you and Lisa find some happiness. Poor Jay was just beginning, and now he'll never have his chance."

I wanted to tell him how angry I was about the Vietnam War and how it now had taken my little brother, but my rantings would serve no purpose.

Lisa was wonderful, and she and my mother embraced as we left. Both of them were crying, and my mother welcomed her to our family.

The next week, Lisa and I were married at city hall in San Francisco. John, Phil, and Sunshine Eagle Feather were the only people in attendance. Phil treated us to dinner at one of our favorite restaurants, then regaled us with stories of famous weddings he had covered in San Francisco, including the day he scooped the competition when he discovered Marilyn Monroe and Joe DiMaggio got married at city hall.

My new bride and I immediately began knitting our lives together as I moved into Lisa's apartment.

A week later, I got a letter from Jay. I think it was written on the last night of his life.

Dear Alex,

Your letters mean so much to me. I appreciate your letters more than I can say. It's like getting in touch with home. I'm so glad to hear that you found someone. Lisa sounds like something special, and I hope it works out for you guys. After all the crap you have had hit you in the last few years, you deserve someone like her.

I can't wait to meet her, if I ever get out of this place in one piece.

We're still playing hide-and-seek games with the VC around these tunnels every night—except they sure as hell aren't games. My unit lost a lot of good guys to these heartless gooks. I hate them. I really hate them.

I'm missing out on football news. I love the fall at home when the Raiders and 49ers and the colleges get going. I need lots of news about the Raiders. This could be the year.

I'm losing daylight, so I have to stop. I hope I can get some much-needed rest tonight and that we don't get shelled again. I miss you, and kiss Lisa for me. I'm missing home tonight. I've got to shake off my melancholy and find some way to survive this madness."

Love you, brother—J

We were told it could take three weeks to get Jay's remains back home and ready to have the graveside ceremony at Arlington National Cemetery.

It was taking longer than usual to get fallen soldiers home and laid to rest because of the heavy casualties coming back from Vietnam. That news made me both sad and angry.

My father was adamant that Jay be given full military honors at Arlington. I believe my mother would have liked a cemetery closer to home so she could visit the graveside. Perhaps this time my dad was right.

I was in regular contact with my parents, and finally, due to their inaction, I booked four flights, got two rooms at a hotel in the capitol, and arranged for a rental car. I decided to just pay the tab to end the uncertainty and confusion. I was just not in the mood for all of this faux drama.

PART THREE

ARLINGTON

27

SAYING GOODBYE

Arlington National Cemetery
October 1968

"We were children of the 1950s and John Kennedy's young stalwarts of the early 1960s. He told the world that Americans would 'pay any price, bear any burden, meet any hardship' in the defense of freedom. We were the down payment on that costly contract, but the man who signed it was not there when we fulfilled his promise. John Kennedy waited for us on a hill in Arlington National Cemetery, and in time, we came by the thousands to fill those slopes with our white marble markers and to ask on the murmur of the wind if that was truly the future he had envisioned for us." – Joseph L. Galloway

It was a chilly, foggy October day at Arlington National Cemetery, when we took Jay to his rest.

Three of us wore black, and my father looked splendid in his Marine dress uniform. Lisa had a large circular black hat, and my mother wore a black veil, very reminiscent of the one Ethel Kennedy wore at Bobby's funeral.

Arlington truly is sacred ground and an emotionally overwhelming experience, even when you are not burying your brother. Since Jay was killed by hostile enemy fire in combat, he was given full military honors.

Lisa and I looked over the misty hillsides at the white headstones that seemed to endlessly into the horizon in all directions before disappearing into the fog. Jay's flag-draped coffin was in a black wagon, which was pulled by a team of six magnificent white horses.

The escort platoon, consisting of four Marines, rode the horses, as my parents, Lisa, and I walked slowly on the winding path through the green cemetery.

The trees and the fog blocked out all sounds except the clop-clop sound of the horses' hooves on the pavement. Like so many things in 1968, Jay's funeral caisson seemed surreal. Yet there was an inevitability to both Robert Kennedy's assassination and Jay's death in Vietnam. We hoped beyond hope that neither event would occur, but the ghostly specter of both tragedies hung over most of the year, despite our attempts to ignore it.

Suddenly the horses halted, and we knew we were at the grave. The very precisely performing pallbearers lifted Jay's casket off of the wagon and gently placed it on the stand over the grave.

Tears ran down my cheeks and Lisa's, while my mother silently wept under the shroud. My father, looking very trim and sharp, stood with red eyes, but his jaw set, showing his determination to not show any emotion.

One of the Arlington chaplains tried to offer some comforting words about eternal life and the ultimate sacrifice made for our country.

A small military band softly played the "Battle Hymn of the Republic." It was a touching surprise to me. I don't know if someone in the family had requested that hymn, but it provided a perfect bookend to Andy Williams' singing of the beloved song at RFK's funeral.

The firing team lined up and began firing a 21-gun salute to my fallen brother. Lisa had her arm through mine and jolted with each shot. After the violence of this year, gunshots seemed wildly inappropriate, despite the military tradition.

The flag off of Jay's casket was presented to my mother, and then a bugler, standing a ways off in the fog, played "Taps."

Suddenly, it was over. We profusely thanked the Marines for a stirring send off for Jay. My father stood at attention, saluting. Lisa put her arm around my mother, and they walked closer to the silver casket. My mother put a flower on Jay's coffin. Tears now started to flow unabated, as I put my hand on the casket and said quietly, "Goodbye, pal. I'm sorry—so sorry. I'll always love you."

The damp chilly weather was starting to take a toll on us all as we stood at Jay's graveside. My parents were offered a ride back to the main building.

Lisa held my mother's hand and walked her to the waiting car. They exchanged an embrace and a kiss on the cheek, but said nothing.

I handed the keys of the rental car to my dad saying, "Why don't you take Mom back to the hotel? Lisa and I will grab a taxi when we're done. I want to stay a little longer."

"Okay, son," Dad said solemnly. "We'll catch up later."

He looked at Lisa's tear-stained cheeks and had a human moment with this new daughter-in-law. "Thanks, Lisa. I wish you'd had a chance to know Jay."

Lisa said softly, "So do I."

As soon as the car whisked my parents away, Lisa and I began to walk up the hill towards the Kennedy graves.

"Do you believe in God?" I asked Lisa.

"I don't know. I've never been very religious, but I can't accept that there's no afterlife. Just look around us," she said, gesturing towards the horizon. "Think of all the young lives that these stones represent. I don't believe their deaths meant nothing. So yes—I think there's a God."

"I sure got religious when I was in Vietnam. I knew a lot of other guys did too. I asked God to help me get home. I think He did, but I don't understand it all. I'm convinced that, for some reason, God helped me live through Vietnam. But why does God allow terrible things like Vietnam to happen? How come I made it and Jay—and several other young guys I got to know—weren't spared?"

Lisa stopped walking. "Look," she said. Through the fog we could see the hundreds of headstones, and across the river, the only thing visible was the Washington Monument poking up through the fog.

"Everyone should come here. They should look at these hillsides and ask themselves, 'Am I sure I want to go to war? Is it worth these lives?' No one wants to hear this or think about it, but my brother died for a lost cause and so have thousands of others in Vietnam."

We stood in reverent silence and then proceeded up the hill, using the barely visible eternal flame on John F. Kennedy's grave as our compass through the misty gloom. We stood at JFK's grave, thinking about all of the history we had witnessed, but I was temporarily confused.

"Where's Bobby's grave?"

Lisa pointed down the slope to a simple white cross. "Right there."

Tears welled up in my eyes, obscuring my vision. I remembered watching the candlelight burial with Lisa in our room at the Ambassador Hotel. It was one of the seminal weekends of my life.

JFK has a grandiose eternal flame. Bobby's final resting place is marked by just a white cross.

Lisa and I moved closer. I knelt down and put my hands on the flat marble grave marker. "Robert Francis Kennedy 1925-1968." Now all the raw emotions gushed out of me. There were tears for Bobby and the cumulative tears for all the tragedy we had experienced in 1968. We wept for him, but also for us.

"Oh, Bobby, we miss you. I'm so sad about what happened. I wish your bullet had hit me. Why couldn't it have hit me? We all need you so badly."

Lisa put her hand on my shoulder and began to quietly sob.

When I left San Francisco to follow Senator Kennedy's campaign around Oregon and California, how could I ever have imagined that six months later I would be standing at RFK's grave in Arlington Cemetery with a tall red-haired woman in black at my side.

In 1968, the nation lost Martin Luther King and Bobby.

I lost Jay.

I lost hope.

Then, I found Lisa.

Robert F. Kennedy's grave in Arlington National Cemetery
(photo by author)

Robert F. Kennedy's grave in Arlington National Cemetery
(photo by author)

AUTHOR'S NOTE

Alexander Hurley is a fictional character and a product of my imagination as are the reporters and editors at the *Associated Press* bureau and the *San Francisco Chronicle*.

Here is the actual list of those wounded by Sirhan Sirhan when he fired eight shots from a .22 caliber Iver-Johnson Cadet revolver just after midnight on June 5, 1968 in the Ambassador Hotel.

- Senator Robert F. Kennedy's wounds included one bullet entering behind his right ear, dispersing fragments throughout his brain. Two other shots hit him—one entered at the rear of his right armpit and another bullet lodged in the back of his neck.
- William Weisel of ABC News was shot in the abdomen
- Paul Schrade of the United Auto Workers union survived being shot in the head
- Democratic Party activist Elizabeth Evans was grazed on the forehead by a bullet as she bent to retrieve a shoe she'd lost in the crowd
- Ira Goldstein, a Continental News Service radio reporter, was shot in the hip
- Teenager Irwin Stroll, a Kennedy campaign volunteer, was shot in the left leg

All of the victims except Senator Kennedy recovered.

Americans Killed in the Vietnam War

Year of Death	Number of Records
1956-1962	78
1963	122
1964	216
1965	1,928
1966	6,350
1967	11,363
1968	16,899
1969	11,780
1970	6,173
1971	2,414
1972	759
1973	69
1974	1
1975	62
After 1975	7
Total	58,220

Vietnam Casualties by Category

(Source: National Archives at <u>archives.gov</u>)

ACCIDENT	9,107
DECLARED DEAD	1,201
DIED OF WOUNDS	5,299
HOMICIDE	236
ILLNESS	938
KILLED IN ACTION	40,934
PRESUMED DEAD (BODY REMAINS RECOVERED)	32
PRESUMED DEAD (BODY REMAINS NOT RECOVERED)	91
SELF-INFLICTED	382
Total Records	58,220

SOME STATISTICS ABOUT THE NAMES
ON THE VIETNAM WALL

Most of the surviving parents of the dead are now deceased themselves. There are 58,267 names now listed on that polished black wall, including those added in 2010.

The names are arranged in the order in which they died by date and within each date the names are alphabetized.

The first known casualty was Richard B. Fitzgibbon, of North Weymouth, Mass., listed by the U.S. Department of Defense as having been killed on June 8, 1956. His name is listed on the Wall with that of his son, Marine Corps Lance Cpl. Richard B. Fitzgibbon III, who was killed on Sept. 7, 1965.

There are three sets of fathers and sons on the Wall.

39,996 on the Wall were just 22 or younger.

The largest age groups, 8,283 were just 19 years old 33,103 were 18 years old.

12 soldiers on the Wall were 17 years old.

5 soldiers on the Wall were 16 years old.

One soldier, PFC Dan Bullock was 15 years old.

997 soldiers were killed on their first day in Vietnam .

1,448 soldiers were killed on their last scheduled day in Vietnam .

31 sets of brothers are on the Wall.

Thirty-one sets of parents lost two of their sons.

54 soldiers on the Wall attended Thomas Edison High School in Philadelphia

8 Women are on the Wall – nursing the wounded.

Source: www.c322association.org/statistics-vietnam.pdf

ALSO BY GREG MESSEL

Follow the writing and news of the author, see trailers and purchase all the books by Greg Messel at his blog at www.gregmessel.com and on Amazon

BOOKS BY GREG MESSEL
Sunbreaks
Expiation
The Illusion of Certainty
Dreams That Never Were

BOOKS IN THE AWARD WINNING SAM SLATER MYSTERY SERIES
Last of the Seals
Deadly Plunge
San Francisco Secrets
Fog City Strangler
Shadows In The Fog
Cable Car Mystery
San Francisco Nights
Face In The Upstairs Window

WISE BEAR DIGITAL BOOK AWARDS NAMED

LAST OF THE SEALS THE BEST SLEUTH BOOK OF 2013

AND DEADLY PLUNGE THE BEST CRIME BOOK OF 2013